CROSSWORD CRIMES

Prakash V. Rao

NOTE: If you purchased this book without a cover, you should know that this book is stolen property. It was reported as "unsold and destroyed" to the publisher, and neither the author nor the publisher has received any payment for this "stripped book."

This is a work of fiction. All the characters and events portrayed in this book are either products of the author's imagination or are used fictitiously.

CROSSWORD CRIMES

Copyright © 2009 by Prakash Rao

All rights reserved, including the right to reproduce this book, or portions thereof, in any form.

www.createspace.com

ISBN: 1449970478
EAN-13: 9781449970475

First Printed by Lulu.com, September 2009
First CreateSpace Edition: December 2009

To my wife, Bhavani, for her constant support, and my boys Ananth and Skanda, who provided the inspiration to go through with this project.

1.	BILLY AT THE NEW SCHOOL	7
2.	INSPIRATION	15
3.	THE TRACK TEAM	27
4.	THE FIRST VICTIM	37
5.	THE CLUE IN THE CROSSWORD	45
6.	THE SECOND VICTIM	55
7.	EMILY JOINS THE SOLVERS	63
8.	PREVIOUS BURGLARIES AND A CONNECTION	71
9.	A VISIT AND ITS CONSEQUENCES	81
10.	THE DANCE	89
11.	PUTTING HEADS TOGETHER	99
12.	A LESSON IN HISTORY	107
13.	CONFRONTATION	115
14.	KIDNAPPED!	123
15.	LIGHT DAWNS UPON BILLY	131
16.	BILLY SPRINGS A TRAP	139
17.	TRIUMPH	149
18.	TYING IT ALL UP	157

1. BILLY AT THE NEW SCHOOL

Greatness is a strange thing. It evades those that seek it and seeks those that evade it. Some people are born great and some become great, while some others have greatness thrust upon them. It is easy to understand being born great – it is simply the chance of being born in a great family. Achieving greatness is another matter. In some, it is the awakening of an overwhelming desire to impress a certain someone with great deeds, or to exact vengeance on injustice meted out either to oneself or a certain someone. It was for these reasons that Billy MacFarlane embarked upon actions that led to great things in his life. In his case, however, it was both the processes of becoming great and having greatness thrust upon him.

Until the time that this story really begins, Billy was quite an ordinary boy, a son of ordinary parents, who went to an ordinary school in the ordinary town of Elmwood. He had ordinary friends, though he was friendlier with some than with others, played ordinary games and enjoyed ordinary things.

Then, as he turned thirteen and entered high school, several things happened. Or, rather, several people happened. The first three were alive, though Billy wished two of them weren't, and the next two were dead. With some quick thinking, Billy prevented more deaths, especially his own. But we're getting ahead of the story here.

#

The first day at a new school is generally full of apprehension, especially if you don't know anyone there. Will other students like me? Will I make friends or enemies? Or will I have to be someone's flunky? What about the teachers? Will they be good to me? Or will there be a dragon waiting to chew my head off?

Billy was lucky in that his best friend from junior high school was with him when he moved to high school. At the least, he had one friend to turn to, to share his experiences with, and to bail him out if he landed in trouble. Not that Billy ever needed that last part. He avoided trouble as best as he could. But he did have something of a temper...

There were others not so lucky. They had to seek hard for that first friend. Emily Richards was one of them. Her family had moved from across the country over summer after her father took on the position of area sales manager for a large computer manufacturer. Emily hated to leave her old friends, but resigned quietly to the inevitable. Not that she had trouble attracting friends – the students flocked to her in droves. No, her trouble was picking the right ones.

Billy saw her on that first day, and longed to talk to her. But his feet took him the other way whenever he caught sight of her. And when he did meet her face-to-face, his tongue twisted so terribly that he thought he'd choke. All he managed were a few unintelligible syllables. He knew it was not polite to stare, but his eyes disobeyed him. He really hadn't noticed girls all that much before. In prior schools, he knew that girls were different from boys, but the difference did not significantly affect him. Moreover, he knew most of the girls in those schools for most of his life and did not think of them as anything other than friends he could play with. Since the town was carved differently for high school assignments, he knew very few girls here. And something inside him awakened to the differences between boys and girls. Especially Emily.

There she was, slim with soft curves, elegant, with clear gray eyes that smiled when her mouth did, and chestnut hair that was cut down to her shoulders.

She had a good complexion, unblemished skin, oval face and almond-like eyes. She was not "glamorous" or even "beautiful". She was pretty and pleasant. And in her pleated red skirt and long-sleeved white silk shirt, she dazzled even more. And intimidated Billy even more.

There he was, skinny with long limbs that flew in every direction as he walked. His clothes, though clean, were crumpled and slovenly. His braces and voice, whose pitch his emerging Adam's apple hadn't quite decided about yet, added to his lack of confidence where Emily was concerned. Billy experienced something new – that strange feeling inside a boy when he first begins noticing girls.

#

On his first day at high school, Billy had good news and bad news. First, the good news: he discovered that he had many classes with Emily (Billy was not quite sure that this was good news – he enjoyed her presence but dreaded the prospect of making an ass of himself before her). Now, the bad news: he had stiff competition – Richard "Rich" Welles, son of a rich local industrialist, began pressing his attentions on Emily at the earliest opportunity. There was more: Sam "Boulder" Sanders, a big, muscular, mean and mealy-mouthed bully demanded Emily's attention. Both Rich and Boulder were used to getting their own way – in their own way! Rich bought his way into anything with his father's money and influence in town, and Boulder flattened all resistance.

There was some hope. When Rich exhibited his exclusive designer clothes, his Gucci shoes and belt, Rolex watch and other signs of his father's wealth, Emily was not among the students (especially girls) who surrounded Rich admiring his possessions (and, in case of the girls, hoping for his favors). And when

Boulder steamed along with his followers – boys who either wanted to avoid his fists or those who wanted to use their own fists from the safety of his shadow, and girls who admired hunks – Emily was not of that number.

#

Billy clashed with Boulder and his gang on the first day of school. It was a simple matter, but Boulder made a mountain out of a molehill. Billy was getting a drink at a water fountain when Boulder came up behind him.

"Get out of my way!" Boulder ordered. "I need a drink."

"I'm not done yet," said Billy.

"Yes, you are now." Boulder pushed him out of the way. Billy, who was leaning over the fountain, fell hard. Boulder laughed harshly. Billy was not taking that lying down! His face turned red as he felt his blood rush to his head.

"You rotten bully!" he screamed. "I'll get you for this!"

Billy rose to his feet and rushed angrily at Boulder. Boulder pushed him back. Three of Boulder's retinue held Billy as Boulder advanced menacingly.

"What's going on here?" asked an authoritative voice. It was the Assistant Principal, Miss Andrews.

"Billy, here, was not allowing me to get a drink," said Boulder.

"I was there first," spluttered Billy. "He pushed me!"

"I'll see you both in my office," said Miss Andrews.

Billy gulped. In trouble, and on the first day at school! What would his parents say?

"Stick to my story if you don't want any trouble," hissed Boulder as they followed Miss Andrews.

"Why should I lie to save your skin?" shot back Billy.

"Quiet!" warned Miss Andrews. She opened the door to her office and waved them in. After seating herself in the straight-backed chair behind the desk, she looked sternly down her long, thin nose at the two boys. She cleared her throat and began.

"A fine beginning," she scolded. "Picking a fight on the first day of school. Let me see now..." She pulled out a couple of files from a filing cabinet. "William MacFarlane, Jr., and Samuel Sanders. Sanders, your record from your previous school indicates that you have a tendency to pick fights. What do you have to say for yourself?"

Boulder lied with practiced ease. "He started it, Miss Andrews. I was takin' a drink of water at the fountain, when he pushed me out of the way."

"That's a lie!" protested Billy. "It was just the opposite..."

"Silence, MacFarlane! You will have your turn."

Miss Andrews' glance took in Boulder's big muscles and Billy's slim frame.

"Do you mean to tell me that MacFarlane attacked you without any provocation from you?" she asked Boulder.

"Yes, Miss Andrews."

"I may be old, Sanders, but I'm not stupid. Neither is MacFarlane – his records show very good grades. He would have to be stupid to attack someone nearly twice his weight, especially while your friends and admirers surrounded you. You will report at the end of the day for detention. As for you, MacFarlane: This is not what I expect from a good student. I will give you a note to take to your parents, and I need their response tomorrow. You may leave us, Sanders. And you, MacFarlane, may sit down while I write this letter."

Boulder left with a malicious grin, as though he didn't care about being given detention whereas he was pleased that Billy was being reprimanded.

After Boulder left, Miss Andrews turned to Billy and asked, "You lost your temper, didn't you?"

Billy nodded in silence, his anxious glances switching between Miss Andrews' eyes.

Billy sat nervously as Miss Andrews scratched her letter. After a few minutes, she looked up and smiled at Billy.

"I have explained everything," she told him pleasantly. "Please give this to your mother with my regards. Helen MacFarlane was one of the best teachers we had here. I do wish she would come back to teach. I taught her, you know, when she studied at this very school."

Billy took the note with some confusion: Had he been punished or hadn't he?

Johnny Wu, his best friend from junior high and the son of his father's partner, was waiting for him outside Miss Andrews' office.

"How did it go?" he asked anxiously.

"I don't know," Billy replied, glancing at the letter he held in his hand. "That bully was given detention. I've been given a note to my parents."

Emily came around the corner and gave him a smile.

"It's all over the school," she said. "You stood up to that bully. I'm glad someone didn't roll over and play dead when he went by."

Billy stared after her. So he did have a chance! He did not have the money to win her with gifts, nor did he have brawn to beat up any competition, but she still noticed him. She made his day. Billy walked about for the rest of the day with a smile on his face, even when Boulder bumped hard into him seemingly by accident.

#

There was one more incident of note on Billy's first day at school. He met Mr. George Smith, the history teacher.

Billy's class contained many serious students. With the exception of the usual quota of bad apples one finds in any class (Boulder and his gang), and the snobs who formed their own exclusive unit with impenetrable walls (Rich and his retinue), Billy quite took to his classmates.

As for the teachers, Billy was lucky with almost all of them. He showed his enthusiasm and his knowledge and evoked appreciation from most of his teachers.

His luck failed in the history class.

Billy was quite good at mathematics and science in general. He could handle anything that required logic, reasoning, understanding, and, to some extent, imagination. He loved solving puzzles of any nature. When it came to memorizing events and dates and names, Billy was out of his league. He saw no purpose in studying things that required no understanding, merely a good memory. Not that he could not do it if he tried - he did possess a wonderful memory. He did not feel the need, and therefore fared miserably in history.

Mr. George Smith was tall, thin, bald, and had a long face with a goatee that made it look even longer. He walked with long strides and a slight stoop. He had a way of shooting his piercing glance from corner to corner about the classroom as though he was a vulture in search of prey. He spoke with a dry, raspy voice and peppered his dry narrative on ancient civilizations with sarcastic comments.

Billy had the misfortune of catching Mr. Smith's attention in his very first history class. It was very simple, really: He fell asleep in class! He didn't exactly lay his head down and begin snoring – he fought it as hard as he could, blinked furiously and rubbed his hands over his eyes. Nevertheless, a seasoned teacher such as George Smith could easily spot the drooping eyelids. He swooped down upon Billy.

"MacFarlane! What was one of the most important contributions to society made by the ancient Phoenicians?"

Billy had no clue. In his efforts to stay awake, he paid very little attention to what really went on in the class.

"No? They introduced the concept of the alphabet. What can you tell us about the democracy of Ancient Greece?"

Billy was silent again.

"They gave the concept of 'One person, one vote', but only free *men* could vote. Tsk, Tsk! What *have* you been doing while I explained all this earlier?"

Billy stared at Mr. Smith with a sad look. Boulder was rolling helplessly on the floor with laughter. Rich smirked. Everyone else in the class grinned. Except Johnny Wu and Emily Richards.

##

2. INSPIRATION

When Billy got home that afternoon, he noticed his father's big car in the driveway. He found his father in the kitchen, sipping a cup of coffee and poring over some papers.

"Home early, Dad?" he asked.

"No, Billy. I just stopped by. I came into the neighborhood while following up on a case."

"Do we have criminals here?"

William "Mac" MacFarlane, Sr., was a detective sergeant with the Elmwood Police Department.

"No, son," he smiled, "just routine questioning. How was your first day at the new school?" Mac generally changed the subject when it got too close to his work.

"Oh, it was okay." Billy did not tell his father about the incident at school. Although Mac was jovial and a sport in everything else, he took breaking rules seriously. The fact was that Billy had not broken any rules – Boulder had pushed him and kicked at him, and Billy did not have a chance to retaliate because Boulders cronies had held him back. But Mac would not see it that way. Anyway, Miss Andrews had asked him to give the note to his mother, not his father. Thank God for little things like that!

"Did you make any new friends?"

"I made a new enemy," Billy thought. "Johnny Wu is in my class," he said out loud.

"That's good. I'm sure Sylvia is pleased with that." Sylvia Wu, Johnny's mother, was Mac's partner. He finished his coffee, picked up his things and headed towards the door. "See you at dinner."

"'Bye, Dad."

Billy waited until his father left before giving his mother the letter from Miss Andrews. She read it in silence while Billy looked anxiously on. She put the letter down and smiled at Billy.

"Now, tell me what *really* happened."

Billy told her about Boulder and the incident at the water fountain. He tried to put the blame entirely on Boulder, but Helen read between the lines. She knew her offspring very well indeed.

"So, you rushed at him in anger," she spoke sharply. "Did you think you could fight him? What do you think might have happened if Miss Andrews had not come along?"

Billy didn't have any answer. He stared at the floor, tears welling in his eyes.

"He would have wiped the floor with you," Helen continued.

"I don't like being picked on," he said hotly. "And I didn't want to take his bullying lying down."

"Billy, I have spoken to you about losing your temper and acting without thinking. Now, look where it has landed you. On your very first day at a new school, at that! You have the rest of the year to go. And more years."

Billy stared at the floor. He felt a big lump in his throat that he could not swallow.

His mother softened and spoke to him kindly.

"It is admirable that you stood up for something. However, you did not stop him. What you have done is worse," his mother explained to him. "You have given that bully a ready victim. His kind loves having a target for his meanness. He will pick on you wherever and whenever possible."

Billy looked worried. "What can I do? How can I stop him?"

"Beat him up."

"WHAT?" Billy almost screamed. "That monster will pulverize me."

"Why didn't you think of that when you attacked him?"

"I didn't think, I guess." Billy looked sheepishly at the best teacher he had ever had.

Helen MacFarlane was a wonderful teacher. Warm and kind, she taught him lessons of life. She smiled indulgently. "Do you see what happens when you act without thinking? Well, there is no point in dwelling on that – we need answers now. I did mean what I said - The only way you can get rid of that bully is to beat him at his own game. Bullies always pick on people weaker than themselves. The moment you beat him up, he will slink away and stop bothering you. You cannot do that now – you are not in any shape to do that. You must train hard. In the meantime, beat him in other things – schoolwork, sports, winning friends, impressing teachers, and things like that."

Billy looked dubious. "How do I train? What do I train in? How can I beat him at his own game?"

"We'll get to that in a minute. Tell me about Boulder. Is he smart?"

"Probably not," Billy scoffed.

"Let me tell you a story about a little boy who was picked on by the school bully. This is a true story: It happened around the middle of the seventeenth century. Now, this little boy was born to a woman whose husband had died only three months earlier. She left this boy at her mother's place and got married again. So, this child grew up without his parents' love. His grandmother was kind but didn't give him the love he needed. He was small for his age, had no friends and most of his schoolmates made fun of him. When this bully kicked him, this boy challenged him to a fight – and won! His teacher watched the fight and encouraged him to beat the bully at studies, too. This boy started working hard, and went on to become a celebrated scientist. Can you guess who this lad was?"

Billy shook his head.

"Sir Isaac Newton," said his mother. "He went on to discover the laws of motion, the law of gravity, calculus and the nature of light."

Billy was awed.

"And all because a bully picked on him at school," she went on. "Do you see what I am getting at? You should not be discouraged by incidents like this. You should turn them around and use them to bring out the best in yourself."

"I have good grades," Billy defended himself.

"Good is not enough, Billy. Be the best. If you become the star student, your teachers and friends will stand up for you. The bully cannot pick on you anymore. Now, about training. You know that your father is a black belt in karate. He has asked you often if you would like to learn karate from him. Why don't you ask him to teach you now? He will be very happy to do so. And if you trained at home instead of elsewhere, you can keep it under wraps until the time comes."

She paused and stroked Billy's hair.

"My child, I have kept you away from martial arts because I don't like violence in general. I am proud of your other qualities, but you do have too quick a temper. I don't want you to learn martial arts just to be able to fight your way out whenever you get angry. I want you to learn to channel your energy, your passion and your temper. Learn martial arts as a discipline, and focus your energy on being the best in whatever you apply yourself at."

#

That evening, after dinner, Billy spoke to his father.

"Dad, I need your help."

"Sure, son. What's up?"

"There's this bully at school who picked on me today. I want to learn to defend myself. Mom asked me to learn karate from you."

Mac smiled at his son. "Billy, it will make me very happy to teach you martial arts. But first, let me ask you something. It takes commitment and dedication to learn martial arts. Are you sure you have the commitment?"

Billy thought first of the bully, and then of Sir Isaac Newton.

"Yes, Dad. I am determined to do something. I will follow it through."

"Good. Now promise me that you will use your skills to defend yourself and the weak, and that you wont attack unnecessarily or just to show off your skills."

"Dad, I am not like that bully. I promise."

So began the training.

#

Early next morning (and I do mean *early*), Billy was shaken awake.

"Uh, where's the fire," he muttered.

"It's time for training, Billy," said his father's voice.

"Dad, it's still dark outside," complained Billy.

"It is 5:30 in the morning. This is the best time to train. You did say you had the commitment and were determined to follow through. I don't see your commitment."

That shook Billy awake. It was like an electric charge passing through his body. Mac knew that the best way to get Billy to do anything was to challenge him.

"I'm ready, Dad," Billy said loudly.

"Good," said Mac. "Remember this, son: Martial arts are not about fighting or physical strength. It is about discipline."

Mac was dressed in sweatpants, tee shirt and running shoes. He had Billy attire similarly.

"There are two things I want to do today. First, let's jog around the block a few times. I want you to build stamina. After we get back, I'll take you down to the basement and teach you how to fall, or break your fall."

Billy started running right away, but Mac stopped him. "Stretches, Billy. I don't want you catching cramps."

Mac taught Billy several basic stretches.

"Relax. Try to undo the knot in you mind. Concentrate on your muscles. If you feel any muscle tense up, try to release it. Try to let a wave of relaxation wash over you."

So they stretched, and ran around their block for a half-hour.

"That's good," said Mac. "Let's not over-do it on the very first day."

Down in the basement, Mac had a little training area with padded mats. He demonstrated to Billy how to roll into a fall, and continue the roll to get back on his feet. Billy tried it a few times until he had the hang of it.

"That's enough for today," called Mac. "Stretch again, and hit the showers. We'll continue tomorrow."

"Do we have to do this so early in the morning, Dad?"

"It's all part of the training, son. Sure, we could do this later in the day. However, I'm trying to build your discipline as well as your strength and technique. Working out in the evening would take away from time you could otherwise use to study or play with your new friends. And I cannot guarantee that I'd be available every evening. I can generally be sure of mornings."

And so they trained in this manner for the next several weeks. Billy soon got used to getting up early in the morning and running in the cool air. After the first week, Mac didn't have to wake him up anymore. Billy awoke much earlier and began his run alone. Mac joined him later.

"You're getting to be a regular runner," remarked Mac after Billy sprinted during the last leg home one day.

"I enjoy it, Dad."

"It may be useful," said Mac with a grin. "You can run away quickly from a battle. Remember, 'He who fights and runs away lives to fight another day.'"

"Dad!" scowled Billy. "I don't want to run away from fights."

"Son, you cannot fight every fight. Learn to pick your fights. You can predict the outcome of a fight before the fight begins, depending on the advantages and disadvantages each fighter has. Look at your fight with the Sanders boy, for instance. If Miss Andrews had not stopped it, you would have been hurt quite badly. You did not have any advantage – weight, strength, technique. All you had was your anger. Now, if you had something to counter his advantages, you can weigh your strengths and weaknesses against his and determine if your something can more than balance his. It's like a chess game – count the number of your pieces covering a position and compare with your opponents' pieces. If you take a pawn with your knight, and he could take your knight with his bishop, see if you can counter that with another piece, or if moving his bishop leaves him at a positional disadvantage. Then, and only then, move to take the pawn. Never get in if it will put you at a disadvantage, either in position or in number of pieces lost for getting something. And do something about that temper of yours. Remember that fools rush in where angels fear to tread."

Billy thought about this. "Dad, it's not only about winning the fight. If I didn't stand up to Boulder, he would have walked all over me. That would have been bad."

"Not necessarily, son. That's what I meant about picking your fights. You need not fight passionately for every issue. For one, people will stop taking you seriously if you react the same way however serious the issue is. You should fight harder for more serious issues and less for less serious issues. If it is an issue is close to your heart, fight for it. If it is an issue that you don't care as much about, ignore it. And, if it is something on the fence, play it by the ear – if the fight is to your advantage, fight it, otherwise, leave it alone. Take the bully's provocation, for instance. Was that really important to you? If you had taken his bullying the last time, he would have had his way and forgotten all about it. Since you defied him, he is not going to forget it. He's going to pick a fight with you whenever possible. By the way, how are you getting along with him these days?"

"Oh, I avoid him whenever I can. He tried to pick on me a couple of times, but I got away."

"Good. Now, let's complete your session for the day and get you off to school."

#

Billy worked hard at his studies so that he could be "untouchable" as his mother had said. Within three weeks, Billy was one of the first students to raise his hand in response to any question asked by any teacher in any class. Well, almost any teacher in

Crossword Crimes

almost any class. He still had a problem with Mr. Smith and his history class.

The problem was not Mr. Smith, although Billy liked to think so. Mr. Smith did tend to pick on Billy, but was well justified in doing so – Billy practically asked to be picked on. He constantly fidgeted in his class, looked out the window, or stole glances at Emily. He did not fall asleep again, but was not attentive even when wide-awake. Poor Billy! It was especially embarrassing to be chastised before Emily. But try as he might, Billy could not pay attention in the history lesson. He had no interest in history. As for Mr. Smith, he had a passion for history and could brook no cavalier attitude towards it from his students.

Billy had strengths elsewhere. He loved anything that challenged his problem-solving skills. He had a strong foundation of fundamental concepts and quickly grasped new ideas quickly. Mr. Edward Martin, the mathematics teacher, frequently called on Billy to work out problems on the board. Billy did so with gusto, much to the envy of many of his classmates. Sometimes, Mr. Martin used particularly difficult problems to play with Billy, but Billy sailed through them easily. Mr. Martin beamed at Billy whenever that happened, and it was the job of both Billy and Mr. Martin to explain the problem to the rest of the class. The verdict was out after the first round of tests – Billy was a shoo-in for an 'A' in math.

The story was similar in other sciences. Especially Physics, the realm of Sir Isaac Newton. He had no problems with languages, either. No, it was only Mr. George Smith and history with irrelevant facts about dead people that kept him from a perfect grade.

Ironically, the best student in history was Emily. And Emily's weakest spot was math. Not that she did badly at math: she was better than the average, but shy of the top. She struggled to keep up with the pace of the lessons.

#

Billy hated having time on his hands with nothing to do. He filled any time he had to spare solving puzzles – of any kind. He was good at most kinds – crosswords, jumbled words, math teasers... all of them. His mother recognized his ability and encouraged it. Quite often, she bought him a book of some sort of puzzle or the other. And Billy solved the whole book within a few days. One day, Johnny found Billy in the quiet of the school library with a stack of puzzle books.

"How do you find time to do them?" he asked. "You must have your schedule filled with all the studying you do to keep at the top."

Billy smiled. "I solve puzzles to take my mind off serious things. I do this whenever I feel saturated and need a break."

"Can I try it?"

"Sure." Billy handed him a book of simple logic puzzles.

Johnny was hooked!

Over the next several days, Johnny spent more time solving puzzles than even Billy did.

"We ought to start a puzzle solving club or something like that," he told Billy one day. "And solve some real puzzles."

"You mean like private detectives?"

"Maybe. Or even things like why something broke so that we can not only fix it but also prevent it from breaking again."

Crossword Crimes

"I don't think many students will join us. The guys are more interested in playing football, or hanging out, or things like that."

"Oh, it could be just the two of us. And we don't have to do this all the time. We could play football, too, or hang out with them."

Billy agreed.

"We ought to call ourselves some cool name," suggested Billy.

"How about the Puzzlers?" Johnny put forth.

"How about the Solvers?" Billy countered. "We could solve any kind of puzzles, riddles, anagrams, problems, things like that. I love doing them all. I like the challenge. That's one of the things that keep my mind sharp, so when it comes to really solving something, I'm in practice. Sherlock Holmes used to play the violin to help him think, but shot himself full of cocaine when he didn't have anything for his brain to work on. I'm not going to do anything like that – I'm going to keep my brain in practice by solving all kinds of problems while waiting for real problems to work on."

Johnny liked the name.

"And so the first meeting of the Solvers will come to order," laughed Billy.

"Yessir, Mr. President, sir," said Vice-President Johnny.

##

3. THE TRACK TEAM

Fall was making itself felt. The trees arrayed themselves in a wide range between a fading green and barren, and all the resplendent colors in between. The sun still shone bright and strong, but the wind demanded a jacket.

It had been over a month since Billy began his training, both in martial arts and in the race to the top of the class. Within a few days of the start of his training, Helen gave him a little present – a short biography of Sir Isaac Newton with anecdotes including the one about the bully and Newton's triumph.

"For inspiration, Billy," she smiled.

Billy carried the book about him all the time. He read it from cover to cover right away. Whenever he could, he opened a page at random and read it. The little book reinforced the pep talk he had received from his mother earlier.

#

Billy bumped in Emily several times – in the corridors, in the cafeteria, on the grounds – and she always smiled at him. Billy always responded with a deep red blush and turned his eyes away.

Emily was generally not alone. Most of the time, she moved around with her friends, a bunch of giggly, chatty girls. Whenever she was alone for an instant, some boy would stumble up to her and stammer a request for a date. Boulder and Rich didn't care whether she was alone or with her friends when they approached her for dates. She never accepted any dates. Her standard response was "I'm busy today".

One Monday, there was a buzz all around school. A big poster had been put up – "Fall Dance Friday". Everyone scurried around to find dates.

#

Boulder came upon Emily in the cafeteria. She was alone at a table, reading a book and munching from a bowl of grapes.

"You're goin' to the dance with me," he asserted.

She looked at him coldly. "You haven't asked me," she said.

"I ain't askin'. I'm tellin' ya." He puffed himself up and swaggered up to her.

"I'm not going with an animal like you, and that's final." She went back to her book.

Boulder was livid. He swept the book and the grapes out of Emily hands, grabbed her wrists and dragged her to her feet.

"No one treats me that way!" he screamed.

"That's because no one else has the courage to stand up to you, you big ape," Emily kept her cool. "You cannot force me to go to the dance with you if I don't want to go with you. Let me go."

"You're goin' to the dance with me, and *that's* final!" Boulder kept his grip on Emily's wrists.

Billy was a witness to all this. He felt the blood rush to his head. He took a running start and cannon-balled into Boulder. Boulder released Emily's wrists to brace himself against the table. Emily fell into her chair. A hush fell over the cafeteria in anticipation of a storm.

Boulder turned to Billy and said in a low, dangerous voice, "Stay out of this if you know what's good for you."

Billy wasn't to be stopped. "Leave her alone, you big bully! If she doesn't want to go with you, you can't make her."

Boulder punched Billy in the face. It took Billy by surprise. He staggered back, steadied himself by holding on to a table, and quickly stepped up to face

Boulder again. A thin trickle of blood rolled down from the corner of his lip, but he didn't care. He looked Boulder defiantly in the eye.

Boulder balled his huge fists and shook them at Billy.

"I can do whatever I want with whoever I want whenever I want. Who's gonna stop me?" he thundered.

"I am," said the stern voice of Miss Andrews. She stood hardly ten feet from Boulder, tall, lean, hair in a tight bun, piercing eyes behind horned-rimmed glasses, and hands on her hips, a formidable figure that meant business. Boulder did a double take, and let his fists fall down to his sides as his jaw dropped open.

"March up to my office right away, Sanders. And you wait outside my office, MacFarlane. While you were right in standing up against oppression, I still do not approve of fighting within these premises."

Billy helped Emily to her feet, and then stooped to pick up her books. The grapes had scattered.

"Are you all right?" he whispered.

"Yes. Thanks." She gave his hand a quick squeeze and smiled at him. "You're bleeding!" She wiped the blood off his face with a napkin. Billy blushed deeply and quickly turned to follow Miss Andrews and Boulder.

Ten minutes later, Boulder came marching out of Miss Andrews' office. He glared at the waiting Billy.

"Five days of detention! It's all your fault. You're gonna get it from me, you watch out!"

"In here, MacFarlane," said Miss Andrews sharply before Billy could find a suitable response. When Billy entered, she waved him into a chair and looked at him sadly.

"I was watching the whole thing, and would have taken care of the whole thing without getting you involved. Now he blames you for the punishment he's getting. It doesn't occur to him that what he did was wrong and deserved punishment anyway. You've made yourself a terrible enemy, Billy. Sam is not the type to forget this easily."

Billy fidgeted uncomfortably. "I just lost my temper when he hurt Emily."

"You have to learn to control that temper of yours, Billy. It landed you in my office before. Granted, on both occasions you were the victim, or helping the victim. However, that bully does not see it that way. You crossed him, so you're his enemy. Your mother wrote to me about your karate training. But you're not ready to tackle him yet. I can protect you from him only if I see him attacking you. Since I cannot be everywhere, and there are many situations in school at any given time, I cannot always be with you. You're pretty much on your own, Billy. Watch out for Sanders. I want you to report this to your mother. Do not think of her as only your mother – she was one of the best teachers here until she decided to start a family. Pick her brains – she'll know what to do. Now, go."

This time, both Emily and Johnny were waiting outside Miss Andrews' office.

"Did you get punished, Billy?" Emily asked anxiously.

"No. She spoke to me about keeping my temper."

"That was very brave of you, Billy, sticking up for me," said Emily. Billy heard his heart thump like a big brass drum. "But be careful. You cannot tackle Sam and his gang."

Crossword Crimes

There was more to come. As the three of them headed back to class, Rich walked up to Emily.

"I'll pick you up at seven on Friday," he said.

"Pick me up?" Emily asked.

"Yeah, for the dance," Rich said.

Emily was enraged. "How dare you take me for granted?" she glared at Rich.

Rich gave her a supercilious look. "Well, I thought I'd do you a favor. I guess you don't know how lucky you are that I picked you for my date."

"Well, you can make some other girl lucky," retorted Emily. "I'm going with Billy."

Rich casually ran his eye over Billy from head to toe.

"*That* Billy?" he sneered.

"Yes, *that* Billy. He has two things you will never have: courage and integrity."

"He can have them. I have money."

"Well, money can't buy me."

As Rich stomped away angrily, Emily turned to Billy.

"Forgive me, Billy. I did the same thing to you that those two creatures did to me – I took you for granted. I didn't ask you." Emily searched his eyes anxiously.

Billy smiled at her. "That's all right, Emily. I'd love to go the dance with you." Billy didn't how these well-articulated words flowed from his lips. He went on. "I didn't dare ask you because I thought you'd go with someone else."

"Do you mean someone like Sam or Rich?"

"Perhaps. I'm not a hunk like Sam, nor rich like Rich. I didn't think you'd go to the dance with a nobody like me."

"You're not a nobody, Billy. Most of us look up to you. You're smart. And honest. And brave. And loyal. I could go on and on, Billy. You have qualities no money can buy and no one can beat out of you. And I'm going to the dance with you because I want to go to the dance with you." And that was that. Emily was a no-nonsense girl!

Billy's heart floated happily for the rest of the day.

#

That evening, he told his mother about all the events that transpired that day. When he told her how Emily picked him to go to the dance with her, and the kind words he received from her, his face turned a bright red. His mother smiled.

"You like Emily, don't you?"

Billy nodded.

"From what you tell me, she sounds like a very nice person. I'd love to meet her. Why don't you call her over someday?"

Billy promised her he would.

#

It had become a game with Billy to find a quiet corner and open the Newton biography to a random page, and then close his eyes and imagine the events on that page. He sometimes imagined himself as one of the participants in the event.

On the Tuesday following his skirmish with Boulder, Billy found a nice spot on the stadium in the school sports arena. While he was in his reverie, he thought he heard Emily's voice call him. "I'm dreaming of Emily," he said to himself. But, when he heard her call him again, he snapped out of his daydream and looked around. She was standing right next to him, smiling.

"Oh, hi Emily!" he said, hastily covering the book.

"What's that you're reading?"

"Oh, this? My mother gave this to me. Newton is my idol," he added proudly. Billy stood up to show Emily the book he got from his mother.

Boulder came up silently behind them. Billy was so intent on showing the book to Emily that he did not notice Boulder until Boulder placed both his palms behind Billy's shoulder blades and shoved hard. Billy went sprawling to the ground, and the book flew out of his grasp. Boulder walked over and picked up the book.

"Well, well!" he gloated. "What an interesting book!"

"Give it back to me!" yelled Billy.

"Make me," Boulder grinned maliciously.

Boulder swaggered towards Billy. Thankfully, none of Boulder's usual group was around, otherwise Billy would have been pinned down by one of them and would not have a chance to escape. Billy knew that although Boulder was big and strong, he was a bit slow in his reaction.

Billy started running towards Boulder. He feinted to the right. Then, as Boulder veered to his left, Billy dropped on his knee, grabbed the book from Boulder's hands, and shot to the left. By the time Boulder turned around and began the chase, Billy had a ten-yard lead.

Billy did not look back. He lowered his head, dug his toes in and kicked off as hard as he could. His training sessions with his father paid off. He heard Boulder's labored breathing behind him – far behind him – while he was breathing easily and regularly. Twenty yards more and he'd be inside the school building. He would be safer there, at least for now.

"MACFARLANE! SANDERS!"

It was Coach Peterson, the track and field coach.

Both Billy and Boulder stopped in their tracks and turned towards the coach. Boulder was almost fifty yards behind Billy.

"Come here!" the coach ordered.

They both walked over, Billy with his hands on his hips, breathing rapidly and taking care to stretch his abdomen to prevent cramping, Boulder doubling over every few feet, coughing and struggling to catch his breath.

"What's this all about?"

"Billy stole my book, sir," said Boulder, between gasps.

"It's my book!" Billy protested. "Boulder grabbed it from me."

Coach Peterson held out his hand. "Let me see the book."

Billy handed the book over. The coach opened it, and there, on the fly-leaf, were the words "To Billy, For Inspiration, Mom". Peterson showed the writing to the two boys. Boulder looked at the words in disbelief.

"Sanders, I will see you after school. MacFarlane, come with me." Score one more for Billy.

Billy followed Coach Peterson into his office by the gym. He was curious. He knew the coach was not going to punish him, because he would have done that already if he so desired. The coach closed the door behind them and waved Billy to a seat while he went behind the desk to a filing cabinet against the wall.

"Do you know how fast you were running, Billy?"

"No, sir." A wave of apprehension swept over Billy. What was the problem now? Did he do something wrong?

"I did not have a stop-watch with me, but you were fairly flying over the ground there. You are not even dressed well for running, and your shoes are not proper track shoes." He paused and beamed down benevolently at Billy. "Billy, you have fine potential. I know it is one thing to be fleeing from a bully and another to run competitively, but I know a good runner when I see one. You have the proper stance and movement. I'd like to time you with proper attire and shoes. We need a sprinter for the league games, and you may well be the ticket."

Billy did not know what to say. "Coach, I've never trained as a runner. I have been running every morning as part of my karate training, but that's different."

"You have the potential, Billy. If you qualify, I'll have Coach Johnson train you. He was a sprinter himself, and is a very patient and dedicated trainer."

Billy agreed to try out the very next day, Wednesday.

Emily was waiting for Billy outside Coach Peterson's office.

"Are you in some kind of trouble, Billy?" Emily asked him.

Billy was touched by her concern. "Far from it," he said. "Coach Peterson wants me to tryout for the track team. He saw me running away from Boulder. He thinks I have a good running style and lots of potential."

"Oh, Billy, that's wonderful!" Emily's face glowed with excitement. Billy felt a warm feeling wash over him as he noted her eyes sparkle.

Boulder was given more detention. And blamed Billy for it.

#

That evening, Billy told his father about the track team. He explained how he concentrated on his running, how he managed to get a jump-start on

Boulder, and how he maintained and increased the lead.

"And if I qualify, I will be trained by Coach Johnson. He was a sprinter, you know."

He was very excited, and his excitement showed. Now he had something to impress Emily with.

Mac beamed at his son.

"I'm proud of you, son," he pronounced.

Billy was elated to receive this praise from his father.

"You were right about running away from fights, Dad. And all the running I've been doing has certainly come in useful."

"It was not only about running away, Billy. It's about picking your fights. You told me about your confrontation with Sam Sanders yesterday – that was a fight you wanted to fight because he was bothering Emily and you didn't like that. When he took your book today, you decided to run away. Isn't it because you thought that the book wasn't worth fighting over with him?"

Billy nodded, surprised at this analysis of his action.

"You have learnt to pick your fights, not to run away."

##

4. THE FIRST VICTIM

Mac made it a point to separate his work from his family. He generally did not discuss cases at home. The most he did was to talk to Helen about specific remarks Sylvia or Captain Ortez, the chief, made. And since they all met quite often on social occasions, this wasn't exactly workplace gossip.

All that was to change.

The entire family was embroiled in the very next case that Mac got involved in. And Mac could no longer separate work and family.

#

The excitement started the next morning when Mac was called away at 2 a.m. to a homicide.

"I would love to be in a warm, cozy bed, too, Mac" said his partner, Detective Sylvia Wu, as she slid into the passenger seat in Mac's Ford Crown Victoria. "The chief wanted us in on this. Seems that there are no real leads to go on."

She quickly gave the gist of the case: The body was found by a cab driver returning from the airport. It would have been missed very easily under normal circumstances – in the ditch on the outside of a curve on a lonely road – except for the fact that the cab driver slept for an instant at the wheel, overshot the turn and almost went off the road. The road is elevated there with a steep slope. He caught sight of the body in his headlights, and called in on his radio.

There were several cars at the crime scene. The area was bathed in the powerful headlamps of the cars and a couple of searchlights that had been setup.

"Ah, there you are," greeted Henry Morrison, the coroner, as Mac and his partner drove up. "I was just getting ready to have the body removed."

"Give us a few minutes, Hank," said Sylvia. The two detectives went down the slope, picking their way and taking care not to disturb the area too much. The going was somewhat difficult because the slope was very steep and full of loose sand and gravel. Sylvia slipped a couple of times and grabbed hold of Mac's arm for stability.

"You shouldn't be doing that in your high-heeled shoes," warned Mac.

"I shouldn't be doing without shoes, either," countered Sylvia. She was right. There were some small, sharp stones mixed in with the sand and gravel that could cut and hurt the soles of her feet.

"If I had known I was going cross-country, I'd have worn my best hiking boots," she complained.

The bottom was covered with grass and weeds.

"Makes for a soft landing in case you slip," said Mac, pointing to the blanket of grass. Sylvia grinned sheepishly.

The victim was wearing what started out as a white shirt. It was splattered with blood, so the white appeared as patches on the red of the blood. The red of the blood contrasted with the white of the shirt and the white of the shirt contrasted starkly against the grass, making for high visibility.

The body was doubled over and lay in a V facing away from the road. Mac and Sylvia walked around and shone their flashlights on the front of the victim. Here, the shirt was relatively spotless, and the white showed clearly.

"The body was still warm when I arrived," the coroner told the detectives. "Rigor mortis had just started setting in. I would say he died around 12:30, give or take a half-hour. I'll call you when I get the slug out of his back. It was a .38."

"Where's the cabbie who found him?" asked Sylvia of no person in particular.

"He went home after giving his statement," a young beat cop replied. "He was pretty shaken up by the experience." He gave Sylvia the statement.

"Seems straight-forward," she said. "He was on his way back from the airport. He had had a long day and overshot the curve in the road. He stopped right at the brink, and picked up the body in the headlights. Look at it – it is highly visible even in the beam from my flashlight."

"What time did he say it was?" asked Mac.

"He puts it at about 1.a.m"

"That's much later than the last flight out. Why was he still at the airport? Where was he? And what was he doing?"

"He didn't say. I guess we need to catch up with him in the morning and tie up loose ends. Don't forget: he was in a state of shock."

"Or so he says."

"That's your policy," smiled Sylvia. "Suspect everybody unless you can rule him or her out."

Mac looked down at the body. "That's a very odd angle," he observed. "If he was shot in the back and fell headlong into the ditch, he would not have crumpled up like that. Unless he was shot elsewhere and thrown into the ditch."

"The bullet missed his heart," said the coroner. "He must have doubled up as he struggled to get back on his feet. He seems to have died of shock, loss of blood and exhaustion rather than by the bullet itself."

"Exhaustion?" Mac was puzzled.

"Look at his pants. There's a streak of blood down each leg. He appears to have been running after he was shot. If he had been standing at the brink when he was shot, he would have slid down or rolled down the slope. That would have left a trail on that sand and gravel. There are no slide marks. You can see that he fell practically at the bottom, almost a twenty-foot drop. There are no powder burns on him to indicate that the force of the bullet impact carried him, and even that would not have carried him so far. Ergo, he was running. His momentum must have carried him all the way to the bottom."

"You stick to being a coroner and leave the detecting to us, Hank" teased Sylvia, knowing how much the coroner loved to dabble with crime.

"If he was running, he may have been warmer than normal. Isn't that right?" asked Mac.

"Right".

"Did your estimate of time take that into account?"

"Yes, and no. The rate at which a body loses its temperature depends on many factors. First, his initial temperature. We know he was warmer than normal due to his running. Second, the temperature outside. I think it is about fifty degrees Fahrenheit. The greater the temperature differential, the faster a body loses heat. Finally, look at his position. He is almost in a fetal position, a position that retains body heat very well."

"In short, you're telling us nothing," piped in Sylvia.

Hank glared at her. "I'm giving you the best estimate I can," he said, hotly.

"I'm not saying you're not, Hank," Sylvia said, soothingly. "You're giving us a range of time he could have actually died. That is not very useful considering he did not die immediately upon being shot. We don't know how far or long he ran, or how long he lay there in exhaustion and loss of blood until he died. He could have been shot anytime. And that makes our job more painful. When and where he was shot? We need those questions answered. Then, perhaps, we can find some witnesses at those places and at those times."

Hank nodded. "I understand the problem this uncertainty causes you. You'd like to narrow your search, and this is not helping you there."

"Any identification on him?" Mac asked the policeman who was the first to arrive on the scene.

"His pockets were empty. Perhaps they were cleaned out. Someone seems to have come down carefully and searched him thoroughly."

"That gives us more questions to answer. Who was he? Who shot him? And, why?"

"I'll give you another question," said Sylvia, quietly. "What's he holding in his fist?" She played the beam from her flashlight onto the victim's left hand. A little tuft of paper showed at the end of the fist.

With some difficulty, and with some help from the coroner, Mac eased a scrap of paper clenched tightly in the stiff fist. He straightened it out and looked at it. "It is a corner torn from a page from a newspaper," he observed.

Sylvia took it from his hand. "Look!" she exclaimed. "It is *tomorrow's* newspaper!"

"Technically today," said Mac, dryly. "It is way past midnight."

"But, don't you see, Mac," Sylvia continued excitedly. "It gives us clues right there. He had access to paper well before it hit the streets. What is the earliest one can get tomorrow's newspaper? That puts the limit on when he was actually shot, even if he only died a couple of hours ago."

Mac mulled over this. They made an odd pair, the big Irishman and little Oriental; the old-fashioned shoe-leather detective and the modern intellectual; the slow, deliberate actions and the quick impulses.

Nevertheless, they worked extremely well together, a well-oiled machine.

"I wonder what was on that page," he mused.

"That shouldn't be difficult. Here's the corner of a crossword. The other side has the end of a comic strip. We can match this to the newspaper. Come on! There's an all-night convenience store that should have the newspaper by now: it is, after all, 3 o'clock in the morning."

"Hold on, Sylvia!" said Mac, sharply. "That can wait a bit. Let's first make sure we found everything this place can yield."

"We can only do so much now, Mac. We need to look at this place in daylight to get more clues. We can meet the cabbie in the morning, and come back later to check for other footprints or tire marks or things like that. And traces of blood along the way, if, as Hank said, he was running for some time before he fell. Now, let's follow up on this single lead we've got."

"I guess you're right," conceded her partner, grudgingly. He turned to Hank.

"Hank, I need a favor from you. When you get the body down to the morgue, get his fingerprints and send them down to Stan Lawson down at headquarters for a match. We must find out who the victim was."

"Sure," said Hank.

The detectives went to find a newspaper, and Hank went down to get the body loaded and transported to the morgue.

#

A half-hour later saw the two sipping coffee at an all night diner and poring over the Elmwood Gazette.

"The comics page or the puzzles page?" asked Sylvia.

Crossword Crimes

"Your guess is as good as mine. The comics look quite ordinary."

"It must have been important enough for him to have been holding it so tightly. Chances are it was still complete in his grasp when whoever cleaned his pockets out wrenched it from his grasp. I wonder why they did not take the body away."

"It may not have been 'they'. It may have been 'he'."

"Or 'she'," piped in the perpetual feminist.

"He was shot once, and did not die right away," Sylvia mused. "His pockets were cleaned out and the newspaper was torn from his grasp. Hank said rigor mortis was just setting in when he arrived at the crime scene. If he had been dead when the newspaper was torn from his hand, his fist would not have been clenched so tightly: the muscles would have relaxed in death before the onset of rigor mortis. Was he alive when he was searched? If so, why wasn't he shot again?"

"He needn't have been alive when the paper was torn. When I tried to extract that piece of paper from his grasp, my problem was not merely rigor mortis, although that was partly the case. The paper was caught in the folds of his fist. And either because of the dew or his sweat, the paper was slightly moist. My problem was getting that paper out without tearing it. That's why I needed Hank's help in prying his fingers open. My guess is that the person who searched him was in some hurry."

"What is so important about a comics page or puzzles page that someone got killed because of it?"

"Copyright violation? Plagiarism?"

"It may not have been something printed on the page. Someone may have used it as scrap paper to scribble notes on it, and that may have been the critical information."

Sylvia shook her head. "I don't know. I think the fact that he had access to a newspaper before it hit the streets is significant."

"I agree. And since, as you mentioned, only the publishers and distributors have access to it early, it does narrow down the list of places he could have gotten it from."

Mac flipped the paper over and looked at both sides.

"Any ideas?"

Sylvia shook her head slowly.

"There's not much to go on."

Mac looked at his watch. "There is not much more we can do tonight. Let's get whatever rest we can."

He dropped her home.

"I'll pick you up about 8 in the morning."

"So much for a girl's beauty sleep," Sylvia sighed.

##

5. THE CLUE IN THE CROSSWORD

When Billy came down for his training session the next morning, he found his father poring over the crossword page.

"Hey, Dad," he said in some surprise, "I've never seen you do crosswords before. What brought that on?"

"I'm not trying to solve crosswords, son. I can't tell you much yet. All I can says is that it relates to a case I'm working on. I'm afraid we cannot train today, son."

"You mean you can solve the case by solving crossword puzzles?"

"I wish it were as simple as that, son," said the big sergeant, little knowing the truth in what he uttered.

Billy took a look at the crossword. "This is simple!" he said. "May I, Dad?"

His father gave him the go-ahead. With practiced ease, Billy filled in a few clues. "That's strange!" he remarked.

"What is?" asked his father, interested.

"Here, take a look at this. Crossword puzzles have words going across from left to right or down from top to bottom. They usually have clues that give you a word starting at the topmost or leftmost square in every group. Here are two groups of squares that don't have a clue to fill the word." He paused. "But I can create a word in those places by solving the clues around them."

A few minutes later, Billy completed the crossword. "Dad," he said, trembling with excitement, "it spells a message! Look! 'Kill Jack'!"

Mac picked up the paper and stared at it. He took the pencil from Billy's hand and circled the words

"Kill" and "Jack" as darkly as he could. "Thanks, Billy! This is a big break on this case. Now, go on and train without me today."

#

Mac called Sylvia. "I'm on to something. I'll pick you up right away," he said.

"I thought you said eight," she grumbled. "It's only seven." Nevertheless, she was ready and looking fresh as a daisy when Mac drove up.

"Don't know how you do it," Mac said with a mix of admiration and envy. "You couldn't have gotten much more sleep than me. I look like something the cat dragged in."

"It's the Oriental way of life, Mac," she replied, brightly. "What're you on to? Why did you take away an hour of my beauty sleep?"

Mac gave her the paper. "Billy solved the puzzle – and found that hidden message."

Sylvia's eyes sparkled with excitement. "Oh, Mac! This is a big break. Let's meet the chief and give him an update. I'm sure he'd like to follow up on this."

"How about meeting the cabbie or checking the crime scene for other prints?"

"We can head to the crime scene right after meeting the chief."

"Hidden messages in the crossword puzzle," exclaimed Captain Rodrigo Ortez. "Someone from the newspaper must be involved here. It fits in with your other comment – if the victim was holding a sheet from today's newspaper yesterday, then there must be some connection with the newspaper or the news distributors. Who else can get their hands on the paper so early? That was a good break we've had here, finding the hidden message. Smart kid you've got there, Mac. Tell him I said so."

Crossword Crimes

Mac and Sylvia decided to split up to follow up on the leads they had. Mac dropped her at her house so that she could pick up her car, and then headed towards the crime scene while Sylvia went to the newspaper publisher.

"Let's meet up at noon," said Mac as he dropped her off. "If you need to get my attention earlier, try the radio."

#

Sylvia asked around the publisher and found that the creator of crossword puzzles for The Elmwood Gazette was G. Fairbanks. Sylvia knocked on the door of the office indicated.

"Who is it?" asked a harried female voice.

"Detective Sylvia Wu of the Elmwood Police Department."

A chair scraped and soft footfalls sounded. The door opened, and Sylvia faced a young woman in her late twenties. Sylvia took in the black tights ending in bare feet, dark green sweater, double strand of faux pearls, and flashing gray eyes in a single glance. She didn't wear much makeup. The woman pushed back her long, dark hair with her left hand, and the diamond on her third finger flashed in the fluorescent light. "No wedding band," noted Sylvia automatically.

"What do you want?" asked the woman with a sigh. "I'm running behind schedule."

"Just a few routine questions, ma'am," said Sylvia, "I'm following up on a homicide."

"Can't it wait?"

"I'm afraid not, ma'am."

"Damn!" said the woman, and let Sylvia in. Sylvia entered a small office with piles of paper all over the place. The woman moved papers off a chair and indicated Sylvia to sit in it.

"How can I help you, Detective?"

Sylvia pulled out a newspaper and showed her the crossword.

"Is this yours?"

The woman peered at the paper.

"That's today's. Let me see now ...That's Paul's puzzle."

"Paul who? I thought you created these puzzles."

"Oh, no, I don't create all the puzzles. I am responsible for the Fun section, and that includes the comics, crosswords, the word search, the maze, and so many more. We get the comics from syndicates. We have a few syndicated puzzles like Jumble and Scrabble. The rest are created in this department. It's not easy, creating 11 puzzles everyday. So, I get some of them from a few different sources. I get crosswords from a couple of sources. That one there is from Paul Samuels."

Sylvia took some notes. "Do you have an address for this Paul Samuels?"

"Here." The woman pulled out a Rolodex and looked it up. She scribbled an address on a yellow sticky note and gave it to Sylvia.

Sylvia wrote some more. "G. Fairbanks. What does G. stand for?"

"Gloria." She said it with a smile that showed perfect teeth and a small dimple.

#

Paul Samuels' office was a small affair in an old, run-down office complex on the outskirts of the main business district. Sylvia felt a bit uneasy about parking her new BMW coupe on the street.

"Wish I had come here with Mac," she thought to herself. "No one will steal his big clunker."

Paul Samuels turned out to be a mousy little man with a toothbrush moustache, buckteeth, and

Crossword Crimes

beady black eyes behind round rimmed glasses. He was only about Sylvia's height and had a small frame. His oily thinning black hair was brushed back. His suit was dirty and crumpled. With a long, straight, thin nose, and long, gaunt face, sweptback ears and a weak chin, his head looked very streamlined. He constantly clenched and unclenched his fists. He peered at Sylvia with a slight squint.

"Yes?" he asked in a high-pitched, nasal voice.

"I'm Detective Sylvia Wu of the Elmwood Police Department. I am following up on a homicide, and have a few routine questions to ask you."

"D-d-d-detective! H-h-homicide!" he squeaked. He turned ashen and swayed on wobbly knees.

"Oh, you have nothing to fear. I just have some routine questions," Sylvia tried to assure him.

However, the little man continued to look horrified. He looked at Sylvia with pathetic eyes while wringing his hands. Sylvia felt sorry for him. She helped him to a chair.

"Do you have something to drink?" she asked him.

He nodded without taking his eyes of Sylvia. He pulled out a flask from his hip pocket and took a swig. His hands shook, and some of the liquor spilled on his clothes. He still had a look of anguish about him, but the firewater he drank brought some color back to his cheeks.

Without wasting much more time, Sylvia got right down to the business at hand. She pulled out the paper she had showed Gloria and smoothed it before Paul.

"Gloria Fairbanks of the Elmwood Gazette told me that you sent this to her."

The little man looked at the crossword and nodded.

"Did you write it?"

"No!" he squeaked, as though it was a crime to be creative and make a crossword puzzle.

"Where did you get it?"

"A messenger brings it over. I then take it to Ms. Fairbanks."

He dwelled on the last word as though he was savoring Gloria's name. Sylvia recognized the lovesickness in him and smiled to herself.

"Poor sap," she thought. "Whom does it come from?" she asked aloud.

"I don't know. Someone brings a cover to me and I sign for it. Then I take the crossword out of the cover and take it to Ms. Fairbanks." Again, he let his tongue roll the name in his mouth before he brought it forth.

"Is that all you do, taking crosswords to Gloria?"

"No, I deliver other things. Things people don't want to know who sent it."

That explained the seedy office and the strategic location at the rim of the business district.

"Do all of them come from the same source with the same messenger?"

"No. Each is different."

"How do you know which goes where?"

"I know by what it is. Sometimes, I get instructions. Sometimes, I get a cover within a cover."

On an impulse, Sylvia pulled out a photograph of the corpse.

"Do you recognize this?" she asked him.

Paul nodded. "He's one of the guys that brought me the crosswords."

"Did he bring one yesterday?"

"No, I didn't have anything for Ms. Fairbanks yesterday." He looked sad about not having an opportunity to meet his goddess!

"Do you have a name for him? Or a messenger service he works for?" asked Sylvia.

"Listen, lady. The folks who deal with me do not use ordinary messenger services. No, I don't know his name or whom he works for. All I know is that he brought me envelopes that I signed for and then left."

"One more question: If you don't know who he is and who is sending the crosswords to you, how do you get paid?"

"I get a hundred-dollar bill pinned to the crossword. This is a cash business, lady. No checks, no credit."

"Quite an expensive service," Sylvia thought as she got back to her car. "But then, there is a price for anonymity. Especially on the other side of the law."

#

In the meantime, Mac had some success at the crime scene. It was much easier to look around in the daytime. It was a bright day with a mild breeze that played with the leaves on the ground.

First, as expected, Mac found the victim's footprints. They were spaced unevenly on the shoulder along the road, and weaving all over the shoulder, suggesting that he was staggering. There were also some drops of blood behind the footprints, indicating that the blood had flowed from the bullet hole down his pants and then dropped off, as Hank had suggested. Mac tracked the prints and blood for about a mile. The blood drops grew smaller, then stopped altogether. The ground was also harder, allowing no footprints. Mac could go no further.

He went back to the crime scene and looked around again. He noted where he and Sylvia went down the night before, and the places where Sylvia slipped. Further off to the side, he found signs of another person who went down the slope and slipped a couple of times - the footprints of the person who went down to empty the victim's pockets? High-heeled woman's shoes! So, Sylvia, the feminist, was right. A woman was involved in all this!

"That may explain why the body wasn't taken away," thought Mac. "She couldn't lift him out of there. So, she had to remove all identification."

He surveyed the area. There was no more information the place could yield. He headed back to rendezvous with Sylvia.

#

Over a quick lunch at a hot dog stand, Mac and Sylvia exchanged information.

"So, the victim was the messenger who brought Gloria Fairbanks crosswords, but not the one he held in his hand while dying," said Mac between mouthfuls. "I wonder why he was killed. Had he stumbled onto the hidden message?"

"We need to find out who he was. Stan and the fingerprint boys may have something."

"Let's stop by at the headquarters before meeting the cab driver."

They went back to police headquarters and checked with Stan Lawson and his crew at the fingerprint section. They were in luck.

"The prints match an ex-con named Jack Keegan who's done time for breaking and entering," said Stan. "He's been out on parole for about eighteen months."

Jack! Was this the intended victim in the crossword message?

"Do you a location for this Jack?" Mac asked.

"The parole officer should have it."

The detectives checked with the parole officer and got the address. Sylvia looked at the address and exclaimed.

"That's a little over a mile from the crime scene. He probably was running away from his home when ... when he fell into that ditch."

Mac agreed. "That's close to where the trail of blood ended. Let's go there after we meet the cab driver."

They met the cab driver but got no more new information. He had been driving late that day because he had had a long day and relaxed a bit at a diner on the way. He felt too tired to drive, so he nodded off a bit in his car right in the parking lot, then headed homewards when it got too cold outside.

The visit to the victim's apartment was very useful. They showed their badges to the superintendent of the apartment complex and gained entry. It was in quite a disarray, with clothes all over the place, the sink full of dirty dishes, and the bed not made up yet.

Sylvia screwed up her nose.

"Disgusting, the way some men live. I don't think any self-respecting woman would let her home fall into such disrepair."

"I don't think he was a self-respecting man, either," said Mac. He believed that it took lack of self-respect to enter a life of crime and lawlessness.

There was some correspondence stacked on the dining table, but was not very useful – standard bills, some of which were past due.

"His wallet is here," said Sylvia. "Has his driving license, cash and cards. That is why there was no identification on the body. The person who went down that slope only got that piece of the newspaper."

"Whoever that was didn't do a good job of it. Which is why you spotted the scrap in his fist, and we found our way here."

The phone was off the hook. Mac placed it back on the hook, took it off after a couple of seconds and hit the redial button. He heard several rings on the other side, and then the metallic voice of an answering machine.

"You have reached the residence of Jack Homer. I cannot take your call right now. Please leave a message after the tone."

Another Jack!

Mac dialed the operator and got the number and address of the last dialed number.

"Now, who was the intended victim?" he wondered, after bringing Sylvia up on this development.

"Another stinking apartment to visit," complained Sylvia.

"It may not be stinking," Mac said defensively. "Not all men let their place of abode become disgusting. Especially if they bring some decent woman to a home-cooked meal once in a while. Don't judge all men by the bad examples."

"Was that a glimpse into your courtship, Mac? Did you treat Helen to home-cooked meals?"

Mac smiled and nodded. Those were some of his fond memories.

They came to the other Jack's apartment. After ringing the bell for a while, they had the superintendent open the door as in the last place.

Mac was wrong. This apartment had a stench as well. But it was the smell of death. Jack Homer lay in his bed with a single bullet wound to his head.

##

6. THE SECOND VICTIM

Sylvia looked at the corpse with horror and screamed. Mac quickly pulled her away into the other room and calmed her down.

"I'm okay, Mac," Sylvia smiled weakly. "It was the suddenness of it all. And the blood and brains everywhere. Oh, it was just horrible."

Mac called in the forensic team.

Captain Ortez came in person to oversee the examination of the second crime scene. Mac was impressed. This usually meant that the captain was giving the case utmost importance.

"Am I off the case, Chief?" he asked.

"Like hell, no!" boomed the big man. "I'm not taking over. This is your case. I have my hands full. The news hounds have gotten wind of two murders in this town on the same night. The mayor's on my rear end to get some answers fast. I told him that you two found this second murder before it was reported. I told him that you are the smartest, sharpest pair of detectives here. Perhaps I oughtn't to have sung your praises so highly. Now he expects the case solved yesterday!"

Mac grinned. He knew what the captain was talking about. The mayor was a political player whose campaign statement was that the crime rate was well under control while he was mayor. In reality, it was under control while Captain Ortez led the department, but the mayor took all the credit for it. And whenever the press sniffed a crime that might blemish the mayor's record, he turned around and put the pressure on the chief of police.

"It's all your fault for having a wonderful record," Mac told Captain Ortez. "Looks like you suffer from a case of Winner's Curse."

Except for the corpse in the bedroom, the apartment was well maintained. And since the corpse was not the fault of the erstwhile resident of the apartment – indeed, the corpse *was* the erstwhile resident! – Sylvia had no cause for complaint as in the other apartment.

The apartment was tastefully decorated. Some of the art pieces that were arranged meticulously were very expensive indeed.

"Here's something interesting," said Sylvia, holding up a file containing bank statements. "This man is – was pretty rich."

"I wonder where he got the money from," said Mac, looking at an antique brass statuette that lay on a highly polished cherry coffee table.

"Not legally, if he was killed because of it."

"Do you see any pay stubs or tax returns, Sylvia?"

"Yes. His tax return shows that he worked for the WhereToGo Travel Company. And listen to this: his bank statement shows that he deposited," she did some quick math, "about four times as much as his tax return shows."

"Very careless of him, blatantly putting that money in a bank account. Well, he's not going to be audited now. That's for sure," Captain Ortez smiled.

This bit of humor was not out of disrespect for the dead but out of a need to relieve the atmosphere when faced with something momentous like death.

"No signs of breaking and entering," observed Mac. "The door's intact and so are all the windows. Whoever entered had a key to this place."

"Or was let in by the victim."

Mac checked the answering machine. The message light was blinking. He called out to the forensic team, "Has the answering machine been dusted for prints?"

"Yes. You can touch it now."

Mac hit the "Play" button.

"Jack, this is Jack Keegan here," came the tinny voice from the machine. "Listen, you've got to get out of town. They are out to get you. I write and solve the messages for the crew. I found orders to kill you."

"The killer must have heard that," said Sylvia. "That may be why Jack Keegan was killed. Well, that solves one mystery – Jack Homer was the intended victim after all. Jack Keegan stuck his nose into it and go shot as a result of it."

"I'm done here, Mac, Sylvia," Hank called from the bedroom. "Come and meet Sleeping Beauty."

"He's no beauty, for sure," muttered Sylvia.

"Do you want to stay here, Sylvia, while I go take a look at the corpse." Mac was really concerned.

"It's okay, Mac. Really. I can take it now. It was just the suddenness of the whole thing."

They went in together. The evidence of the victim's wealth was everywhere - in the stereo system against the wall, in the matched mahogany bedroom set, in the white satin sheets on the bed and in the cream pajamas the victim wore. The bedroom was tastefully decorated.

Hank gave the tour. The victim had been shot in the right temple – the side nearest the door - at very close quarters. There were powder burns all over the right side of his face. A portion of the left side of the face – and head – was a mess. Blood and brains caked that side of the bed, and scattered as far as the wall about ten feet away.

"Was he drugged before being shot? How else could someone have come as close as that without him putting up a struggle?" asked Mac.

"I'll confirm when I give you the results of the autopsy and blood test, but my guess is that he was dead drunk."

"That's strange. I don't see any evidence of drinking. No bottles, no glasses. Everything is put away neat and tidy."

"There's more," said Bob Hart of the forensics team. "There's not many fingerprints around, not even the victim's. Someone has gone to great lengths to remove evidence of his or her presence here."

"That would imply that the killer's presence was not normal here. We need to find out who, among the victim's circle of acquaintances, would not come down to his apartment."

"That explains why there is no evidence of breaking and entering. The victim knew the killer. He must have let him or her in."

"Then he or she killed Jack, tidied up the place, did the dirty dishes and put them away, then left."

"Very decent of the killer, wouldn't you say?" piped in the captain. His walrus moustache quivered in his mirth. "What we have here is a clean criminal. A pity the body was left in so much of a mess."

Sylvia managed a smile. "If the other Jack had been killed in his apartment instead of on the road, the killer would have probably cleaned that place, too, and left it much neater than we saw it."

"With things so neat and tidy, would you say the killer was a woman?" Mac asked Sylvia jokingly.

Sylvia fixed him a look.

"I remember you telling me not long ago that not all men were untidy like Jack Keegan, and that some were actually neat."

They all laughed and went out together. Mac and Sylvia headed towards WhereToGo Travel Company while the rest returned to headquarters.

Crossword Crimes

#

WhereToGo Travel Company turned out to be a small office on the first floor of a busy shopping complex in the center of town. The glass front display contained many posters of bikini beaches, palm trees, cruise ships, and other promotions.

"Call us when you want to know Where To Go" claimed the slogan under the store name.

It was a busy place. It was well located near the watering holes in the shopping mall, and the advertisements were strategically placed to attract attention.

When Mac and Sylvia walked in, an attractive platinum blonde in a short purple designer dress suit walked up to them. She had an almost perfectly circular face framed in short, straight hair that hung close, pert upturned nose and hazy gray eyes. She parted her lips in a smile that showed perfect teeth.

"Can I help you?" she asked in a sugary voice.

Sylvia and Mac flashed their badges. Her expression changed from expectation to disappointment.

"What do you want?" she asked in a flat voice.

"Can we talk privately, ma'am?" Mac asked

"We can go into my office." She led the way. "I don't have too much time. One of my employees did not come in today. He didn't even call in. This is a very busy time of the year. I am short handed."

Mac nodded. "I know. Jack Homer."

She stopped and stared at him.

"How do you know that? Is ... Is Jack all right?"

"Let's go into your office, ma'am."

She turned around and led the way, looking back at them several times apprehensively. She let the detectives in, waved them to seats and closed the door behind them. She sat down across the table from them and looked directly into Mac's eyes, waiting for him to speak.

"I have bad news, ma'am," he began.

"Caroline," she interrupted.

"I beg your pardon?"

"Please don't address me as 'ma'am'," she flashed a quick smile. "It makes me feel too old!"

"Caroline ... what?" Mac asked.

"Caroline Fallace."

"I have bad news, Ms. Fallace," Mac began again. "We found Jack Homer dead in his apartment."

"Oh, Lord!" she cried out.

Her hands flew to her mouth. Tears began welling in her large, expressive eyes. Sylvia walked up to her and put an arm around her. Caroline looked up gratefully at Sylvia. She reached out and grabbed a couple of Kleenex tissues, and carefully daubed her eyes without damaging her mascara too much.

"Was he ... did he die ... of natural causes?" she asked anxiously. From her questioning, it appeared that she expected the worst. Why? Sylvia wondered.

"No, ma'am ... Ms. Fallace. He was killed. Shot. Do you know anyone who may have wanted to kill him?"

"No," she protested. "Jack is ... was a wonderful person. I cannot think of anyone who might want to kill him."

"Did he have any special friends?"

"Well, he used to date a couple of girls who work here. I ... I've dated him several times myself. Although he's ... was my employee, I felt he was special so I allowed him the privilege of dating me, although I didn't do it too frequently."

"Did you visit him at his apartment?"

"Yes. A couple of times."

"Can I have the names of the other girls whom he dated?"

"Yes. Let me see ... Karen Johnson. She's the red-haired girl to the right of the entrance. And Maria Bellini. She's the receptionist."

"Could we question them, Ms. Fallace?"

"Yes. You can use this office. I'll send them in. Do you have any more questions for me?"

"Yes." Sylvia took up the questioning. "We looked into to his files and found that he made much more money than he showed on his tax return. Do you know where that could be from?"

"Well ... He did gamble a bit," she conceded.

"He'd have to back long shots and win consistently to make the kind of money he did. Anything else you can think of?"

"I don't know if he moonlighted and worked for anyone else. He may not have had the time to do that, though. He had a date almost every night. He was that kind of person."

"Whatever that kind of person might be", thought Sylvia.

"Did he only date the three of you, or could he have had other female acquaintances?" asked Mac

"It is possible he dated others." Caroline nodded. "I ... I don't know for sure."

Karen Johnson was quietly beautiful. She had a pleasant face, gentle brown eyes and a generous mouth. She wore a simple brown suit and very little makeup. She sat very upright in Caroline's seat with her hands in her lap and looked directly at Mac and Sylvia when they spoke to her.

She took Jack's death well. She registered shock but showed little emotion.

"I'm sorry for Jack," she said quietly. "He always wanted to have a wonderful time."

She couldn't add anything more to what Caroline said. She had visited Jack at his apartment.

Maria Bellini was glamorous. She had jet-black hair and eyes, and used plenty of makeup although not garishly. She wore a colorful, flowery frock and plenty of jewelry.

She broke down when she heard of Jack's death. Sylvia put an arm around her, comforting her.

"Oh, Jack! Oh, Jack!" she kept repeating.

She couldn't add to Caroline's statements either. She had visited Jack at his apartment, too.

Mac had a final question for Caroline.

"Do you know if Jack had any family around here?"

"He didn't talk about his parents. They're divorced, and he is quite angry with them about it. He has a sister in Milwaukee. I think she inherits everything he had. I'll contact them all and let them know Jack is dead." She sighed wearily.

Mac thanked her, and the two detectives left.

##

7. EMILY JOINS THE SOLVERS

Meanwhile, Billy had quite an eventful day.

At the earliest opportunity that he had, Billy pulled Emily and Johnny into an empty classroom and told them about the crossword puzzle. His friends were very excited.

"I think there are more hidden messages in crosswords," said Billy. "Would you like to help me solve the crosswords in the back issues?"

"Where would you find them?" asked Johnny.

"In the Elmwood Public Library, of course," said Emily. "Let's do it after school today."

Billy groaned. He'd promised to meet Coach Peterson to time his sprinting and see if he'd qualify for the track team. He told the other two.

"That's okay, Billy," Emily said. "We can do it after you have had your tryout. It's not going to take long, is it?"

"I hope not," he replied.

#

At the end of the school day, Billy reported to Coach Peterson. The coach directed him to wear a tracksuit and spiked running shoes. They went out to the track. Coach Johnson stood ready at a finish line they had prepared with a stopwatch in his hand. He waved out to the two of them when they arrived. Emily and Johnny waved from where they were watching from the stands.

"We're only going to see if you qualify. That means that we are not timing you exactly. If you get to the finish line within twelve seconds, you qualify. Got that?"

"Got it!"

"Ready, Billy?" Coach Peterson asked.

"Give me a couple of minutes, Coach," said Billy. As his father had trained him to do, he stretched and relaxed his muscles. He closed his eyes and concentrated on letting a wave of relaxation flow through him.

"Ready!" he said.

"On my mark, run to Coach Johnson. I will signal by blowing on my whistle."

Billy took the sprinter's position on the starting block and looked straight ahead.

Coach Peterson blew his whistle and waved a flag at the same time. Coach Johnson started the stopwatch.

Billy concentrated on getting the maximum forward motion from every stride. He regulated his breathing and cut the air with his hands to counter his feet. He concentrated his very being on the thin ribbon that lay ahead of him, oblivious to all else. And met the ribbon with his chest.

He slowed to a walk, concentrating on his breathing and relaxing his abdomen. He walked back to Coach Johnson.

"Well done, Billy! You covered 100 yards in less than 12 seconds. You made the cut-off. With training, you can shave tenths and hundredths from your time and win races."

Emily and Johnny walked over, cheering Billy. Coach Peterson walked over, too, and he had a big grin on his face.

"That League Sprinting Cup has your name on it this year, Billy," he said. "I would like you to train every day after school. I'll work it out with Miss Andrews."

Billy savored this moment with a proud smile.

After he showered and got back into his regular clothes, he met Emily and Johnny to get to the library.

Crossword Crimes 65

The three of them sped on their bikes, and within minutes they got to the Elmwood Public Library.

"This looks like a perfect case for the Solvers!" said Johnny.

"What are the Solvers?" asked Emily.

Billy explained. "Would you like to join us, Emily?" he asked with some hesitation.

"Oh, I'd love to!" said Emily enthusiastically. Billy was extremely glad to hear that.

As they entered the library, Billy asked the librarian where they could find previous issues of the Elmwood Gazette.

"We're researching into something that happened recently," he told her. She pointed them to the newspaper archives.

"Recent issues are in this binder. Older issues are on microfiche."

"We only need the recent issues for now," said Billy.

After she left them, Billy turned to the other two.

"We cannot write on them, so solve the clues on a piece of scrap paper. Then solve the hidden words by taking appropriate letters and stringing them together. You don't need to solve the entire puzzle, just around the hidden words."

Within a half-hour, they had solved ten past puzzles and found the hidden words. The eleventh puzzle didn't have any hidden words. They stopped there.

Billy wrote down the hidden messages on a notepad.

The hidden words were, from the most recent to the least:

"Jack", "Will", "Squeal"
"Not", "More"

"Jack", "Wants", "More"
"Loot", "Split"
"Hill", "Top", "Job", "Done"
"Hill", "Top", "Today"
"Cando", "Hill", "Top"
"Case", "Hill", "Top"
"Two", "Weeks"
"Seven", "Hill", "Top", "Ave"

"What does it mean?" asked Johnny.

"Look at it from the oldest," said Billy. "The first is an address. The second is a length of time. And look at the last! That shows why today's message was issued. Jack, whoever he was, was not happy with his share of the loot and was going to squeal on them. Come on, let's show this to my dad and your mom, Johnny!"

#

The three of them rode over to the police headquarters. Billy knew his way around, and the desk sergeant who knew Billy let them by. Billy found his father writing up his report on his visit to the travel agency.

"Dad, I have something to show you," he said.

"Is it too important to wait until I get home tonight?"

"Yes, Dad. It tells you why Jack was killed."

Whatever Mac was expecting, this wasn't it. He stopped whatever he was doing, and turned and faced Billy. Seeing that Billy was dead serious, not merely playing a joke on him, he got to his feet and looked around for Sylvia. He saw her near the water fountain, talking to Captain Ortez.

"Sylvia! Chief! Over here!"

He found an empty interrogation room and herded the youngsters into it. Sylvia and the captain followed. Mac closed the door after the last of them filed in.

Billy displayed the scraps of paper.

"We went to the library," he told them, "and solved previous crosswords to find hidden words. We stopped at the first puzzle that had no hidden words."

Mac put them in order.

"The first is an address. The second is a length of time. The third instructs someone to case the joint."

"What does casing a joint mean, Dad?"

"That means looking over the place to see if it can be broken into, whether it would be worthwhile doing so. Let's see ... the fourth looks like a report that it can be done. See the 'cando'? That stands for 'can do', two words. That means that it can be done. The fifth is a command – 'Do it today'. The sixth says that it was done. Hmmm ... That was five days ago. I wonder why the crime was not reported yet. And then there are reports that the loot was split, that Jack wanted more, and that he would squeal if he did not get more, finally instructions to kill Jack. That was today. Poor Jack! Like Oliver Twist, he wanted more. And see what happened when Oliver asked for more. People ought to learn from that, don't you think?"

"Perhaps you should go down to 7 Hilltop Avenue and check it out," said Captain Ortez.

"Can we go along, Dad?"

"No, you kids go home. You've done quite a lot for the day. But," he stopped them, "don't go around trying to find other pieces of information. There have been two killings already. I want you to be very careful. The killer does not appear to have any qualms about killing."

As the three rode away, it dawned upon Billy that he hadn't told his father yet about qualifying for the track team. Oh, well. This could wait until he returned home.

#

Hilltop Avenue was in a classy section of Elmwood. Seven Hilltop Avenue was a large mansion with large grounds, a wall and wrought iron gates.

"I don't have to case a joint like this if I was a burglar," said Sylvia. "If I knew for sure that I could get in and out without a problem, I would surely rob it."

The gate was on wheels and was probably opened remotely. There was a button, a microphone and speaker on one side of the gate. Mac pressed the bell several times with no avail.

"Nobody's home," he observed.

"Do you want to get in?"

"Let's look around first."

They walked down to one end of the wall. Number Five, the adjoining house, was not walled in. Instead, there was a hedge around it. Mac walked to a gap in the hedge and squeezed in. The yard sloped upwards. The wall around Number Seven was not a constant height above the ground. It stayed level with the front for a while and stepped up gradually with the slope. As a result, there were places where it wasn't much of a wall.

"That's how the burglars hopped in," Mac thought. He squeezed back out of the fence and the two detectives went around to the front door of Number Five. When Sylvia rang the bell, a young girl about Emily's age answered it.

"Hi!" she said, brightly.

"Good Evening, Miss," Mac greeted her. "We're from the police." He flashed his badge. "Do you know if the people next door are in town?"

"Number Seven? No, they are on vacation. We have the keys if you want to go in. We generally leave our keys there, too, in case of emergency."

"We don't have a warrant to enter the premises. If your parents can permit us, we can check around without the need for a warrant."

"What are you looking for?"

"We think the place has been broken into."

"Really? Let me get my mother. Mom!" She went inside.

"Who is it, dear?" A pleasant looking woman in about her mid-thirties appeared. She was casually dressed in tights and a long T-shirt, and had a novel in her hand.

"These people are from the police department, mom. They think Number Seven may have been burgled. Do you want to take a look?"

"Number Seven has a good security system. How can it be broken into?"

She went to a desk in the hall and took out a set of keys.

"Follow me," she called, and went towards the back of the house. The detectives and the girl followed her.

Introductions were made along the way.

"I'm Maureen Tucker. This is my daughter, Barbara."

"Detective Sergeant William MacFarlane, and my partner Detective Sylvia Wu."

They went out onto the back porch. There, beyond the swimming pool, was a little door in the wall leading into the next yard. Maureen selected a key and opened the door, then led the way to a French window. She selected another key from her bunch and opened the French window. Soon upon entry, she punched a code into a keypad and disabled the security system.

A red light above the keypad steadily blinked a pattern. Two quick flashes, a long pause, a long flash, another pause and then the pattern repeated.

"That's not right," said Maureen. She flipped open the keypad and pulled out a piece of paper. This was a chart to interpret the blinking pattern.

"There has been a power outage! The security system had been down for a while and reset itself! Barbara, go get your dad! Quickly!"

"And call the police," added Sylvia. She fished out a card. "Here, call this number. Ask for Captain Ortez. Tell him Sylvia Wu asked you to call him."

Ten minutes later, the place was crawling with policemen and representatives of the home security system trying to determine how the system was breached.

"It is difficult to determine what exactly was taken," said Captain Ortez. We need the owners of the house here."

"They've taken a two week vacation. They left about ten days ago. They went on a cruise, so they cannot get here much sooner than a couple of days."

Two weeks! That was the second message, the length of time. And the first one was ten days ago! The detectives looked at each other, then at Captain Ortez.

"This fits with the messages in the crosswords," exclaimed Sylvia, her eyes sparkling with excitement.

"This is another crime that you've found without it being reported. That's quite a smart lad you have there, Mac. You must be proud of him."

"I am, chief. Very proud of him."

##

8. PREVIOUS BURGLARIES AND A CONNECTION

The next morning, Billy and his father resumed their training sessions.

"These sessions are as good for me as they are for you, Billy," Mac confessed. "I know the value of practicing everyday in order to keep up my skills, but I don't do it as regularly as I would like. I can blame my work schedule, but it boils down to a tiny amount of laziness that grows and grows until finally I am not practicing at all. Teaching you is forcing me to keep in practice. They do say that teaching reinforces learning, and I fully agree. I am completing my own learning by teaching you."

Billy told his father about making it into the track team.

"The training really paid off, Dad!" he exclaimed. "I relaxed as you taught me to, the concentrated every ounce of my energy into each step I took. It was a wonderful feeling."

Mac looked at his son bursting with pride.

"Like I told you, son, martial arts is not about fighting or physical strength. It is about discipline. I am glad you're learning those lessons as well as the moves I am teaching you. Remember this: I can teach you techniques, but it is up to you to apply those techniques. I can teach you how to fight, but you have to analyze the situation and decide whether you should fight or not. There is an old English saying 'He who fights and runs away lives to fight another day'. The Chinese teacher of war, Sun-Tzu, said that the outcome of a battle is determined before the battle even begins. It is all in the training and discipline of the soldiers, in the use of diversion and deception, in the choice of battle ground, in the preparation and use of weapons, really, in every tiny thing. Anything can be used as a weapon if used right."

Billy was to remember these words very shortly. These words saved his life.

Mac told him in turn about the disabled burglar alarm at Seven Hilltop Avenue.

"The owners were on vacation for two weeks. Starting ten days ago. It's all there in the hidden words you discovered in the crosswords. The Captain thinks you're the best thing that happened to this case. That still does not give you the go-ahead to put yourself in danger."

#

Considering that Billy's primary concern was defending himself from Boulder, Mac had initially taught Billy defensive techniques.

"There is no point in launching an offensive if there is a hole in your defense," he explained.

After teaching Billy how to roll into a fall to avoid getting hurt, Mac taught him how to stabilize his stance so as to not fall or be pushed over, but also to be able to flow into another stance if the need arose. Then, he taught him defenses.

The first defense was avoidance.

"Your eyes must be fast enough to determine where whatever is directed at you will land. And wherever that is, no part of you must be there. Try to always present a small target to your opponent. That reduces the chances of getting hit."

He pelted Billy with tiny rubber balls from a large gun that used air pressure to propel them. Initially, Billy got hit quite a lot and yelped frequently. As the days passed, Billy got pretty good at avoiding the little speeders.

"Good," said Mac, one day after Billy totally avoided getting hit. "Now, in real life, you cannot always avoid getting hit by moving because you may not have the space to move. The next step is to deflect something coming at you."

He gave Billy two little paddles, one for each hand, and taught him how to use them.

"Don't go across your body. Deflect the ball using the closest hand. Always move your hand away from the body. Position the paddle first to be in the line of the ball's motion, don't try going across the line. Going across the line requires much greater speed and timing."

Again, Billy failed initially and felt the pain. Over time, he learnt to follow the ball very quickly, and position the paddles well in time to deflect them.

"This is just physics, Dad," he explained. "Laws of conservation of momentum. And leverage. I read all this in the Newton book."

The last of these techniques was using defense as a form of offense.

"Try to direct the balls back to me," said Mac. "Put pressure on your opponent, don't give him enough time to draw a bead on you."

Finally, on the day after Billy solved the first hidden messages in the crosswords, Mac taught him basic punches and kicks.

"Don't hit at something, Billy. Hit through it. At the point of impact, your fist or leg must be moving at its highest speed."

Mac let Billy practice by himself while he practiced some of his more complex moves. Billy stole a glance at him between his punches and marveled at how light that big man was on his feet, and how quickly he moved.

#

During the history lesson, Billy kept thinking about the case. Mr. George Smith kept up a dry narrative about William the Conqueror and the Normandy Conquest. He noticed Billy's dreamy look and perceived his lack of attention. He swooped down upon Billy as a wolf upon the fold and began making an example of him.

"MacFarlane, when was the Normandy Conquest?"

"I ... Well ... Er ..."

"What was the significance of the Normandy Conquest?"

Here, Billy simply shook his head and looked sadly at Mr. Smith. Mr. Smith was without mercy.

"I have heard say you are star student, MacFarlane, but I am yet to be impressed by your scholarship. You will write a ten-page report on the Normandy Conquest and its significance and hand that in for the next class. The rest of the class will have no assignments this time."

As soon as Mr. Smith left the classroom, Boulder gave a loud whoop.

"That's worth ten detentions any day," he declared.

Billy glared at Boulder. "You're pathetic!" he said, at last.

"No, you are!" said Boulder. And danced a little jig around Billy.

"Don't let that bully upset you, Billy," said Emily, while they walked down to the next class. "I can help you with that stuff. I know all about the Normandy Conquest. And the report is not due until Monday. We have the weekend to work on it."

"If we don't spend that time solving puzzles," said Billy. He told her about the house on Hilltop Avenue and the disabled security system. "I think there's more information to find in the newspapers."

"What shall we solve today?" asked Emily excitedly.

"I have an idea. Let's meet after my track practice. I'll get Johnny as well. I don't want to wait until the owners of that house get back from their vacation."

#

Emily and Johnny eagerly waited for Billy to finish his track training and join them.

"Where to?" asked Emily, as they picked up their bikes.

"Back to the library. I don't think this is an isolated case. I think these burglars have been doing this for some time. I want to find the addresses of the previous places they broke into, and then ask the owners of those houses some questions."

"What kind of questions?" asked Johnny.

"Well, who would know when you're going away and for how long?"

Emily considered this. "What would I do if I went on a vacation? I would ask the post office to hold the mail, then I would stop the newspaper for the duration of time, and then I would pay any bills that come due. If I had a pet, I would find someone to care for the pet."

"That's a good start," said Billy. "I would also like to know where the victims went on their vacation, and how they traveled. I am looking for anything that might be a common link between them."

"Where do we start?"

"Like I said, let's go to the library and find the addresses of the previous burglaries. We can then go to those addresses and ask some questions. We can pretend we're taking a survey for our school project. Say, how frequently they go on vacation, where they went the last time, what do they do to prepare to go on vacations, things like that."

"We'll have to solve hundreds of puzzles to do that," complained Johnny.

"No, we don't. Do you remember what we did last time? We stopped as soon as we found a crossword with no hidden messages. It is easy to spot whether a crossword has a hidden message or not – just look for all the pivotal squares and see if they correspond to a clue or not. What we have to do today is to find the first crossword that has a hidden message after a series of crosswords without hidden messages."

"Do you think that'll work?" asked Emily, impressed with Billy's reasoning.

"Not always. Remember how they work? Someone gives an address and a length of time, the boss says case the joint, then, after whomever cases the joint says it can be done, the boss gives the go-ahead to do it. If we only look for addresses, the first ones after blanks, not all the addresses we find may have been burglarized. But it will be a lot easier to find."

"But we will have more houses to survey."

Billy frowned. "You're right. Well, let's find a few addresses first. Then, we can decide what to do about them."

They asked the librarian to help them use the microfiche reader. Emily and Billy looked at the microfiche, while Johnny looked at the last of the recent newspapers in the binder.

An hour later, Emily put down her pencil and rubbed her eyes. Billy took her lead and stretched.

"This is tough going," he said. "We've gone back about nine months and only found three addresses."

"That's a good start," said Johnny. "Let's go and visit them."

Emily was the voice of conscience of the group. "Didn't your father ask you not to take risks? There have been two killings already."

"I wonder who the second was," said Billy. Since Mac did not bring him up to speed on the case, the youngsters did not know about the two Jacks. "Anyway, we are not going to the killers. We are only looking at the victims. That ought to be safe."

The first house was a large house in a cul-de-sac that contained similar houses. Billy rang the doorbell.

"Who is it?" asked a gruff voice from within.

"We're doing a survey for a school project, sir," said Emily, in her sweetest voice.

A tall, pot-bellied man opened the door. He wore faded jeans and a dirty T-shirt of no particular color that barely covered his paunch. His white hair was messy, and he had a bottle of beer in his hand.

"Survey, hey? Make it quick: I'm watching my favorite show. You have until the commercial break's over."

"How often do you go on vacations?" Emily asked the first one.

"About once a year. But we won't be going for a while. Not since our house was broken into the last time."

"Oh, I'm sorry to hear that," said Billy quickly, although he was secretly pleased about finding a victim on the first go around. "Where had you been?"

"We went on a package cruise to the Caribbean."

"When was that?"

"About two months ago." This matched the date on the newspaper they had found the hidden address on.

"Who were your travel agents?"

"Let me see now ... WhereToGo. They are in the big mall in the center of town. There's a slick salesman – Jack Horner or something. Nice guy, but slick."

Jack! They were on the right track.

"This is the most important question on our survey, sir," Johnny took up the questioning. "What do you do in preparation for a vacation?"

"I see what you're getting at." The man smiled. "Your school is teaching you proper safety procedures. Well, we generally have the mail held, stop our newspaper, and ask our neighbors to take care of the houseplants. The next time, I'm also going to make sure everything is either tied down so those darn burglars can't get their hands on it, or make sure it is insured to the hilt!" He managed a wan smile.

"Thank you, sir," they all chorused.

They rode excitedly to the next one. It was one half of a two-family house.

"What do you think?" Johnny asked Billy.

"Chances are it has not been burgled. I see now why the gang cased joints before they took action. Do you think we should ask them where they went on their vacation?"

"Good idea," said Emily.

They heard yells and screams from the house as they approached it. Billy rang the bell again. A young woman with a couple of small children in tow opened the door. She had on an apron and carried soup ladle.

"Yes?" she asked. "If you're selling anything, I'm not buying."

Crossword Crimes 79

"Sorry to disturb you, ma'am," said Billy, politely. "May we ask you a couple of quick questions for school project we're doing."

"Make it very quick," she said, wiping her free hand on her apron. "I have something on the stove."

"How often do you take vacations?"

"About once a year."

"When and where did you go on the last one?"

"Let's see ... about four months ago. My husband and I left the children with my mother and went on a two week cruise in the Caribbean." The dates matched, and she went to the same place as the previous people!

"Who were your travel agents?" Emily asked.

"Oh, is that what you're surveying? We had that nice man from WhereToGo Travel Company – Jack Homer. He had a wonderful way about him." She blushed when she said that.

"Thank you, ma'am." They did not need to ask anything more.

"Don't you think it is curious?" remarked Billy as they rode to the last address. "The man in the first house called the travel agent Jack 'slick', and the woman in that last house called him 'nice'."

"I think it is normal," said Emily. "She found him attractive – she blushed when she mentioned him. Jack may have been very attentive, and that's something a woman likes very much. If it was a woman travel agent, the man would have found her attractive and the woman would have called her something else, probably 'vixen' or 'a tramp'."

The last address led to a fairly large house near their school. They heard the shrill barks of a small dog when Billy rang the bell.

"Down, Precious!" called a female voice as the door opened a crack. The children positioned themselves to be visible to whoever was behind the door. "What is it?" she asked.

"We're taking a survey for a school project, ma'am," said Emily. "Can we ask you a few questions about the last vacation you took?"

"Oh, yes. Come in, children. I'll hold Precious back."

She opened the door, and let the three of them enter. She was quite young, perhaps in her early-twenties. She was blonde, and very beautiful. Johnny ogled at her, and blushed deeply as she smiled at him. She wore a short, sleeveless red evening dress as though she was ready to go out somewhere.

"When did you take your last vacation?" Emily asked. Johnny was too tongue-tied to ask anything.

"About two years ago."

Billy was surprised. "Didn't you take one this year? About eight months ago?"

"Oh, no! I've been at this house only for a few weeks. And my ..." She paused and took in the young faces before she resumed. "My friend bought this house about six months ago. It had gone on auction. Something to do with a bankruptcy."

"That must have been the burglary," thought Billy. "Another case of insufficient insurance. Or, maybe not all their money was legal."

"Do you have any plans for a vacation soon?" Billy asked bravely.

"Oh, I hope so. I want to spend a few weeks on the Riviera, but my friend works so hard, I don't know when he'll have the time for me. Do you have any more questions? I need to get going – I'm meeting him for dinner at a classy joint tonight."

They didn't have any more questions for the woman. They thanked her and left.

##

9. A VISIT AND ITS CONSEQUENCES

"Where next?" asked Emily.

Billy was silent. He was thinking.

"This is making sense," he said, at last.

"It is?" Emily and Johnny both wore a puzzled expression.

"Sure. Who would know when someone went on a cruise? And how long they would be gone for? The travel agency! I'll bet every last penny I have that Jack Homer made all the travel arrangements for all the victims. Let's go and see WhereToGo Travel Company."

Emily was not for the idea.

"Billy, you know that your father did not want you to get into trouble. It's one thing to survey victims, but another to go to the killers," she admonished.

"We need not go in," said Billy, excitedly. "We can just see the place from the outside."

Reluctantly, Emily followed Billy to the downtown shopping mall. The three Solvers looked up the mall directory and found the travel agency without much trouble. They saw posters of bikini beaches, palm trees and the cruise ships in the window display.

"Look!" said Johnny. "Caribbean cruises!" He pointed to the display.

Billy looked at the display with interest.

"They run about once in two months. That seems to be the frequency of the burglaries. We've had one now, one two months ago – that was that man who didn't have enough insurance. We didn't have one four months ago, but there was a potential victim. That was that woman with a couple of kids who found Jack very attractive. And then six months ago, those people in that big house went bankrupt. I think that was related to a burglary, too."

An attractive platinum blonde in a short, blue designer dress suit walked up to them.

"Good evening, you kids. Are you trying to figure out where to go when the weather gets cold here?" she asked them pleasantly.

Johnny's eyes grew wide and his jaw dropped. This one was even more beautiful than the one in that big house!

"We're looking for Jack Homer," he blurted out the first thing that came to his head. Billy and Emily groaned and looked at each other.

The woman froze in her tracks. Her smile faded, and a puzzled expression appeared.

"He's no longer with us," she said. "Why do you want to meet him?"

Billy tried to salvage the situation.

"Several people we spoke to said that they had bought their Caribbean cruise vacation package from him."

"I can help you with that. I'm Caroline Fallace. I own this travel agency. What are your names?"

"I'm Billy MacFarlane."

"Emily Richards."

"J-Johnny Wu."

Something stirred in Caroline's memory. She looked at Billy and Johnny carefully.

"Are your parents in the police department? This is about Jack's murder, isn't it? Well, tell those busybodies I have really told them all I know about it, and they can't pump more information from me by sending the cute little kids!"

She stalked off, angrily.

Johnny stared after with a pained expression on his face. "They didn't send us," he called out. "We're here on our own. We're just asking around about Jack. Sort of ... play detectives."

Caroline stopped and turned around. She opened her mouth as though she was going to say something and then stopped.

"Go away," she said wearily. "Just go away!"

"That does it!" said Emily. "We must meet your Dad and tell him everything. And your mom, Johnny."

"I think he might be at home about now. Let's look for him there."

#

They found Mac at home.

"Dad, we have something to tell you," said Billy. Emily and Johnny stood a few feet behind him.

"What have you found now?"

"More burglaries. These people have been going at it for a while. And we found a connection. WhereToGo Travel Agency!"

"How did you find them? And the connection?"

Mac was impressed. Three children were on the same track as two seasoned detectives!

"We went to the library and looked into crossword puzzles for the past six months. We found addresses in the hidden messages, and went and talked to the owners. We found that two of the three addresses we found had been broken into. And all when they were on a Caribbean Cruise. And all of them had the same travel agent. Jack Homer at WhereToGo Travel. When we went to the travel agency, the lady there guessed that Johnny and I are sons of cops, so she wouldn't talk to us."

Mac heard Billy out in silence. He got up and paced around a bit.

"You put me in a very difficult position, the three of you. I have already told you that I don't want you to endanger yourselves. I appreciate your efforts and enthusiasm. However, fighting crime is not a game. It is not only about solving puzzles. There's real danger here. What you did in the library is all right. I can even accept your talking to the victims. You ought to have come to me directly after that. Now someone knows that you've been asking questions not only about the burglaries but also about Jack Homer. If she spreads that around and it gets to the wrong ears, you kids may be in serious trouble."

Emily looked at Billy with an "I told you so" expression on her face.

"It was my fault, Mr. MacFarlane, sir," said Johnny. "I spoke to that lady. I ... I couldn't help myself. I ... I took one look at her and wanted to tell her everything I knew."

Billy stopped him.

"It's my fault, Dad," he said, looking directly into his father's eyes. "I convinced them to take a look at WhereToGo."

"I'm glad you're accepting the responsibility, son," said Mac. "It's very easy to find someone to lay the blame on. It is much harder to take ownership of mistakes. Success has many fathers. Failures are orphans. Everyone jumps in to take credit for a successful operation. Everyone shies away from a failure. There's a story about a general during the Second World War. He was called in to answer some questions from a panel trying to determine whom to honor for a particular victory. He told them that he didn't know who should take credit for the operation, but they were looking at the person they'd have court-martialed if it had failed."

Helen took pity on the three forlorn faces.

"It's dinner time. Why don't you two have dinner here, Emily and Johnny? You can call your homes and let them know you're here. We'll walk you home after that."

They ate in silence, each with his or her thoughts on all that transpired. After dinner, Billy and Mac walked the other two to their homes.

#

Later that evening, Mac spoke to Billy.

"I've just been discussing with Captain Ortez and Sylvia. I'll bring you up to speed on the case, son, because you deserve it. You've helped a lot. But I don't want you spreading the information around because it is privileged – we haven't cracked the case yet. Promise me you wont tell anyone."

"Can I tell Johnny and Emily, Dad?"

"Only if they make the same promise, and keep it."

Billy promised his father he would keep the information he received confidential.

Mac told him about the two Jacks, the footprints in the sand at the first crime scene, the lack of prints at the second one, the message on the answering machine, and the girls at the travel agency. He also filled Billy in on what Sylvia found at the newspaper, and from Paul Samuels.

"We also did some checking up on unsolved burglaries in the past. There have been about seven unsolved burglaries over the past eighteen months. Those two addresses you found match up with two entries on the list. We are up against a major operation here."

Eighteen months! Billy thought of something.

"Dad, how long did you say the first Jack was on parole?"

Mac looked up. They were onto something.

"Why, that was eighteen months!"

"And did you say that his message on the other Jack's answering machine said that he was the person who wrote and decoded crosswords for the crew?"

"That's right! He might have been one of the brains behind the operation."

"Here's something I don't understand, Dad. If Jack Homer was providing all leads to potential victims, why kill him? Isn't that like killing the goose that laid golden eggs?"

"Unless they found another goose or other geese that laid golden eggs." Mac thought back about the girls at the travel agency. Was one of them the new informant?

"And how about Jack Keegan? If he was one of the brains behind the operation, why kill him?"

Now, that was a poser.

"What if the killer didn't know which Jack to kill and so killed both anyway?" suggested Billy.

"That makes the killer stupid and with no sensitivity."

"How do you mean?"

"If, as you suggested, the killer killed both Jacks because he or she was not sure which Jack he or she was supposed to kill, and killed both just to be safe, the killer would have to be stupid and insensitive. Stupid, because if he or she wasn't stupid, the first thing he or she would do is to confirm which Jack before going on a killing spree. Insensitive is what one would have to be in order to kill two people instead of one. Killing is not easy, son. It takes a lot to take someone's life and look at the lifeless body. That act takes saps one's spirit. Especially the body of Jack Homer. That was a ghastly sight. Now, if someone can do that, and go traipsing to Jack Keegan's apartment to kill him just because he or she did not know which Jack to kill ... Well, let's hope that that person is not here for long. We certainly don't want a senseless killer in our community."

"You keep saying 'he or she'. Do you think it could be a woman?"

"We don't know for sure. It may not be a woman. At the least, Jack Homer's murder was very brutal, and women are generally not so brutal. However, we did find a woman's footprints near Jack Keegan's body, so we know that a woman was involved. We don't know too much yet."

"We know something," declared Billy. "We know that Jack Homer was the intended victim because of Jack Keegan's message on the answering machine. We know why Jack Homer was killed – he didn't like his share of the loot, and threatened to squeal if he didn't get more. We don't know why Jack Keegan was killed."

"Ah! Don't jump to that conclusion. We *think* we know why Jack Homer was killed. We don't know anything for a fact. We're going by those messages you found in the crossword puzzles. Now, suppose it wasn't more money or a greater share of the loot that Jack Homer wanted. Suppose he wanted a bigger role in the gang. After all, he did start the process – his information led to the burglaries. True, he only did his job. And perhaps he did not take risks. But the information he passed must have made many rich. Perhaps he was tired of being a mere cog on a wheel. Perhaps he wanted to be a big wheel himself."

Billy looked puzzled.

"That's another thing. He threatened to squeal. Whom would he squeal to? The police would have clapped him in irons. And if he squealed, he would be another one that killed a goose that laid golden eggs. Did he have another option?"

"Perhaps he was going to give the information to another gang. A rival gang. That way he wouldn't be killing any geese, just switching geese. Perhaps that's why he was killed. We may be in the middle of a gang war here. That's another reason why your action today was dangerous. Your goose may be cooked. And that's not one that laid golden eggs, either," Mac grinned.

"I'm confused, Dad. Is this how you detectives operate, coming up with various scenarios until you have no idea where you are?"

"No, son. I was trying to impress on you that it is not easy. When you started listing things that you thought we *knew* for a fact, I wanted to bring you back to reality. We do have a very good idea about what could have happened. We have come a long way in this case, and part of the credit goes to you. But nothing has been verified. And until it is verified, you should not go about claiming certain knowledge."

Billy was humbled.

"I guess I got carried away. Only, it seemed so easy to put things together."

Mac looked at his watch.

"It's late now. Off to bed," said Mac. "I'll see you bright-eyed and bushy-tailed first thing in the morning."

##

10. THE DANCE

The next day was Friday, the day of the dance. Billy was in a highly excited state all day.

"Whom are you going with, Johnny?" he asked his best friend.

"I don't know," said Johnny. "I haven't screwed up the courage to ask anyone."

"To tell you the truth," said Billy, "if Emily hadn't asked me, I wouldn't have anyone to go with either."

But he felt sorry for his friend. When he sat next to Emily at lunch (which he had been doing since they fixed their date), he asked her if she knew any girl who hadn't found a date yet.

"Let me see ... I don't think anyone has asked Liz Chen yet."

"Johnny feels too tongue-tied to ask any girl. Do you think you can get Liz to ask him?"

"I'll do better than that. Why don't you go find Johnny? I'll get Liz and meet you back here."

Ten minutes later, the four of them met in the cafeteria. Emily was to the point.

"Johnny, meet Liz Chen. Liz, meet Johnny Wu. You're going the ball with each other."

And that was that! How simple she made it! Billy couldn't have done.

Johnny and Liz were stunned. They looked at Emily. Then they looked at each other. And, suddenly, all the four of them burst into laughter.

"She's not as beautiful as Caroline Fallace," teased Billy, "but you shouldn't complain."

"Who's Caroline Fallace?" asked Liz, interested.

"Oh, nobody!" said Johnny, quickly, blushing a violent red.

"She's someone we met at a travel agency yesterday," explained Emily with a grin, "and Johnny had a crush on her."

Liz giggled. "Thanks! I can use that when I need to get his attention."

Johnny laughed good-humoredly.

"I'll get you yet," he told Billy.

"Emily, may I pick you a bit early?" Billy asked her. "My Mom was quite impressed with what I had told her about you, and what little she saw of you yesterday. She wants to say something to you."

"Okay."

#

Billy got to her home at six. He wore a light sports jacket and one of his father's ties, and carried a small box of candy. He was nervous as he rang the doorbell.

"Ah! Yes. Billy MacFarlane," said Emily's father, as he opened the door for Billy. "Emily's told me some wonderful things about you. Come on in and take some weight off your feet. She's not ready yet."

Billy went in and sat where he was indicated.

David Richards was a large, jovial man. He had white hair that he swept back, and short, well groomed beard and moustache. His eyes twinkled merrily behind rimless glasses. In his left hand, he held a pipe that he used for pointing to emphasize his well-articulated words. Billy took to him instantly.

"Emily tells me that you're in the track team," he boomed. "That's good. Myself, I was into shot put, discus throwing, and things like that."

Billy could well believe that, seeing the rippling muscles on the big man.

"Do you still keep in shape, sir?"

"I wish I did," said Mr. Richards, ruefully staring at his waistline. "I push some weights, play some racquetball and golf, but nothing like the old days."

Emily came down at that moment. She wore a simple, yet stunning blue dress. Billy stared at her almost in disbelief, while her father wore a proud expression that seemed to say, "Yes, that's my girl!"

Billy got to his feet and tentatively presented the box of candy to Emily. She accepted it quite naturally and made Billy feel comfortable.

"Thanks, Billy! Shall we leave?"

"Curfew time is ten o'clock, Billy," said David Richards good-naturedly.

Billy nodded. The two youngsters left and headed towards Billy's house.

Helen received Emily warmly.

"Come in, dear," she said gently. "After hearing wonderful things about you, and meeting with you yesterday, I wanted to share something with you. Come, sit with me."

She sat with her on the couch and indicated Billy to go away. She spoke to Emily very gently.

"Billy told me how you stood up to the local bully and weren't impressed by the riches of the local spoilt brat. I think those are wonderful qualities. In my time, too, there were bullies and brats. In fact, the fathers of the two you are now facing in your day – George Sanders and Bart Welles. History is repeating itself, which is why I am telling you this. I picked Mac because of his principles and simplicity. He stood up to the bully, too, and helped me when the bully bothered me. I turned down the rich kid, too, and he never forgave me for that. He has caused me much grief, but I overcame all that. I see that a second generation of Sanders and Welles are causing the same problems. I called you here to tell you that if you ever feel unsure of yourself, if you ever feel pressured into doing things your conscience tells you not to, and if you ever need to turn to someone for support and comfort, you can always come to me."

Emily's eyes moistened. She hugged Helen tightly and shook as she suppressed her emotions.

"Thank you very much, Mrs. MacFarlane," she said, at last. "It is wonderful to have someone like you watch over me. My mother died two years ago. My father is wonderful – kind, gentle, caring, supportive, generous, loving. But he can never completely replace a woman. And there are times when a girl needs a woman to talk to. I really missed my mother."

Helen nodded understandingly.

"I didn't realize that your mother's no more. I'm very sorry to hear that. Again, if there's anything I can do for you, do ask. It is wonderful that your father is someone you can look up to. A girl needs a stable influence from such a figure. That is another thing about Billy's father. He is someone I look up to, and proudly. He has been in Elmwood all his life, just as I was. Yet, there is a quality about him that will fit in a small town as well as in a big metropolis. He joined the police force because he felt strongly about fighting for justice. One of his heroes in his youth was a policeman who lived in our neighborhood. That kind man taught Mac very practical lessons in life, just as Mac and I are teaching Billy. I wish I could teach Billy about keeping his temper."

"I think Billy has many wonderful qualities," said Emily, loyally. "He has told me that you are a wonderful teacher."

Helen smiled. "You're a wonderful girl, too, dear," she said, gently. "You have qualities that should make your father very proud. You know where your loyalties lie, and have a very sound conscience."

She gave Emily a quick hug and brushed her lips on the girl's head.

"Now, go," she said, kindly. "I think Billy is very anxious to show you off at the dance."

#

Shortly after, Billy and Emily left to go to the dance. Billy proudly took her by the hand as heads turned to look at the dazzling Emily. She felt radiant after her meeting with Helen MacFarlane. They found Johnny and Liz and went over to them.

It was a wonderful atmosphere. Music and laughter filled the air. When the band struck up the next number, Emily turned to Billy.

"Shall we?" she asked.

"I don't know how to dance," Billy confessed to Emily.

"Let's do an easy step," Emily suggested. "Just feel the music, and move to your feelings. I'll do the rest."

They went out to the floor when the music started. Billy listened to a few bars of the music. He held her hands and looked into her eyes. Emily smiled and moved with the music. He took her lead and moved, first very self-consciously, then gradually with abandon. He felt elated. He'd never felt anything like this before.

When the music stopped, it took Billy by surprise. Emily laughed happily at his expression.

"The music must stop sometime."

Billy didn't want the music or the dancing to stop. He could go on forever.

After a few dances, Emily wanted a break.

"I'm not a runner like you, Billy. I don't have your stamina. I'd love to keep dancing, but my legs cannot go on forever."

They headed towards the punch bowl. Billy poured Emily and himself some punch. Then it happened.

Rich Welles walked up to Emily.

"I'll have the next dance, Emily," he said, coolly. "Let me show you some real dance steps."

He sneered at Billy. "I have a proper pair of feet, not two left feet!"

Billy felt his face flush. He was about to retort, when Emily gently squeezed his hand as if to say, "It's all right. I can handle this."

"No, Rich, I am not dancing with you."

Rich turned livid.

"You can't turn me down," he said angrily. "Nobody turns me down and gets away with it."

"Grow up, Rich. You cannot always get your own way."

"I'll get my way. Or else."

"Or else what?"

"My Dad has a lot of money and influence in this town. I can get your dad out of his job, and you out of this school. Do you still refuse to dance with me?"

"Yes, I still refuse. Your dad may be rich and powerful, but you're nothing. In fact, you're less than nothing – you have nothing of your own. You don't even stand on your own two feet. You're propped up by your father. You're in your father's shadow, and you'll always remain there."

"You'll pay for this! I'll see that you do!"

Rich angrily swept a cup off the punch table at Emily, drenching her with punch.

"What's happening here?" asked a stern voice. The ubiquitous Miss Andrews loomed at Rich's elbow.

"I slipped, Miss Andrews," said Rich, glibly.

Again Billy made as if to retort, and again Emily stopped him.

Miss Andrews looked at Emily's dress.

"You poor thing! Apologize to Emily, Welles!"

Richard apologized – or, at least, he said the words, although his eyes sent a different message. "That's what happen to people who cross me!" his eyes seemed to say.

After Rich and Miss Andrews moved out of earshot, Emily turned to Billy.

"Let it go, Billy," she said.

"But, your beautiful dress," Billy spluttered. "He's ruined it."

"Billy, that brat is used to getting his way or throwing tantrums. He probably breaks his toys when he is angry. He did just that today. As for my dress, it doesn't matter. Really! I've had a wonderful evening, first with your mother, and then dancing with you. Don't let that brat spoil this mood with his tantrums. Come on! Walk me home. I'll change my dress, and we can walk around in the mall."

Billy couldn't help smiling back at Emily when she put her face close to his and looked earnestly into his eyes. They went back to Emily's house, as she suggested.

"Back already?" asked her father, quite surprised. "You still have lots of time to spare on the curfew."

"We had a little mishap, Dad," Emily said quickly. "I spilt punch down my dress. I'll change into something casual, and we'll go down to the mall to hang out."

"Give me just a minute," she called to Billy, as she ran up the stairs.

Billy settled back, prepared for a long wait, but she came down almost immediately afterwards.

They went down to the mall and had a wonderful time. Billy saw everything again for the first time with her, sharing her excitement and joy.

Finally, when Billy dropped Emily off at her home, they stopped outside the door and looked hesitantly at each other. After what seemed like an eternity, Emily leaned forward and kissed him on the cheek.

"Good night, Billy. I'll pop over in the morning."

She gave him a quick smile, turned around and walked in.

Billy's heart soared a million miles above the earth.

"Good night, sweet Emily!" he said softly.

He walked back home tipsily.

Emily looked in on her father before she went up to her room. She told him what Billy's mother had told her.

"I'm very happy for you Emily. I was worried about bringing up a girl all by myself, especially at an age when your body and mind are going through so many changes. You've turned out wonderfully, and I'm glad Mrs. MacFarlane is helping you. I will look in on her one of these days and thank her."

"Dad, I don't think you ought to worry. You've done a terrific job of bringing me up. You've always been there for me, and that counts more with me than anything else in the world. True, sometimes a girl needs a woman to talk to, someone who understands what it is to be a girl and go through the things I am going through. That is the only thing that you cannot do for me. In all else, you've been both a mom and a dad to me. I love you very much, Daddy."

"I love you, my precious Princess!"

Emily hugged her father tightly, kissed him, and went up to her room.

David stared at a large portrait over the mantelpiece. It contained him, Emily, and an older version of Emily.

"She's turned out after you, Angela," he said to the woman in the portrait. "She's going to be just as wonderful as you."

"What a wonderful day it's been!" Emily exclaimed as she got to bed. Images of her father, Helen, Billy, and all the people who loved her floated past her mind's eye. She lay in bed with a happy smile until sleep finally overcame her.

##

11. PUTTING HEADS TOGETHER

The next morning, Mac was preoccupied through most of the karate training session. Billy was dying to ask him about the case, but held himself back. His father did not usually bring his work home, and spoke as little about his cases as he could. He might not appreciate questions about the case.

Finally, as they finished up and headed up from the basement, Billy couldn't contain himself anymore.

"What's happening with the crossword case, Dad?"

Mac shook himself out of his thoughts and stared blankly at Billy.

Billy repeated his question.

"Nothing much, son," he said, finally. "We haven't made any more progress since Thursday. Mind you, we've gone much farther than with the other unsolved burglaries. We've found the link between all of them – the Caribbean cruise. But with Jack Homer dead, all the other girls at the travel agency are stoutly disclaiming any involvement with anything that may have led to his death. Here's what happened yesterday. We've got a ballistics match between the bullet that we dug out of Jack Keegan and the bullet that was found in the wall in Jack Homer's bedroom. Those came from the same .38. Then, Sylvia and I sifted through Jack Homer's papers and things with no luck. He deposited cash into the bank in used bills, and that's not easily traceable. Nobody looks at serial numbers on banknotes unless there's something wrong. He was careful enough to deposit small amounts over long periods of time to allay suspicion. None of the stuff in his apartment came from any of the burglaries. We have gone over all the clues very carefully. What we have is a mere coincidence – he arranged the cruises, the addresses of the travelers appeared as hidden words on the day they left on the cruises, within a few days the houses were broken into. There is nothing to pin it on Jack. Gloria Fairbanks of the Elmwood Gazette did not name Jack as one of her sources. She only named Paul Samuels. I don't know if she knew of the existence of Jack Homer or Jack Keegan."

"Did she ever name the other source?"

"No, she didn't. She couldn't. When Sylvia asked about her that yesterday, she said that someone at the newspaper left a message in her inbox one day. The message said that the person was interested in creating crosswords but wished to remain anonymous. She was happy to accept them – what with all the puzzles she needs to create, she would take any help she could get. She replied to the anonymous letter as she was instructed to do, and received crosswords occasionally since."

"Did she ever receive more than one puzzle the same day? If so, which one would she choose?"

"That's an interesting question. I'll ask her."

Billy thought for a while.

"Dad, those puzzles came from *three* sources, not two. Jack Homer was one – he sent the first two in any set giving the address and the length of time. The others were a set of instructions and reports. If, as Caroline Fallace said, Jack had a date every night, he couldn't have carried out the instructions. Is it possible to find out whom Jack Homer dated on which night going back about two weeks?"

"I'll ask the girls at the travel agency. What are you looking for?"

"Gaps. And which messages those gaps coincided with. We assume, based on the travel agency connection, that he sent the first messages with the address and date. What other roles could he have played? Another possibility is that he dated one girl coincident with one set of messages, so the girl was an accomplice."

"Could he have *given* the instructions?"

"It is possible, but not likely. It all depends on whether he had the time to do it, and that comes back to finding the gaps in his dates. Then again, why would he threaten exposure if he was the person giving instructions. Can you find out from Gloria which crossword came from which source? Some sort of cross-reference? You don't need all of them – just the past three weeks should do."

"What do you want to do with that cross-reference?"

"Here's my take on it: The internal source at the paper is probably the big boss, giving instructions. The two Jacks were probably the other sources who gave Gloria the crosswords through Paul Samuels."

"That's a thought," said Mac. "Let me see what Paul has to say."

"He may not tell you anything. That's why he is paid more than any other courier – he probably gets paid for his silence."

"I wish there was a way of getting information out of him. Do you have any other thoughts, son?"

Billy was thrilled by that question. "Are you really asking me for help solving the case, Dad?" he asked with a grin.

"Considering you gave us the first big breaks early in the case, I would say you've been part of the team all along. Now, do you have any other thoughts?"

Billy thought for a while.

"I have two thoughts, Dad. First, Paul Samuels did recognize Jack Keegan's photo and picked him as one of the sources of crossword messages. Can you show him Jack Homer's photo and see if he recognizes it? And can you find out from him how many others sent crossword messages to Gloria Fairbanks? We don't need to know who, just how many."

"I'll look into that. What's the other one?"

"How did they break into the houses? Did all those houses have security systems? Did they have different security systems or where they all from the same company? If they all had the same security system, that would be another common link. Another thing: Jack Keegan had been in jail for breaking and entering. Do you know how he broke into houses?"

"Good thoughts, Billy," his dad said encouragingly. "I'll get all of that, and we'll put our heads together again. After all, two heads are better than one."

"I'll call Emily and Johnny, too," volunteered Billy. "That makes four heads."

"Sure. And I'll call Sylvia. Five heads are a lot better than one."

#

Later that afternoon, the five of them got together around the MacFarlane kitchen table.

Mac started off the discussion. "I have a list of the crosswords and Gloria's answers as to their sources."

He checked them off.

"'Seven, Hill Top Ave' and 'Two Weeks' came from Paul. 'Case Hill Top' came from the internal source. 'Cando Hill Top' – Paul. 'Hill Top Today' – internal. 'Hill Top Job Done' – Paul. 'Loot Split' – Paul. 'Jack Wants More' – Paul. 'Not More' – internal. 'Jack Will Squeal' – Paul. Finally, 'Kill Jack' – internal."

"Orders were from the internal source. Everything else came from Paul," observed Billy.

"Yes, you were right about that, son," said Mac. "It appears Jack couldn't have been giving instructions. Unless he was leading a double life, which, we were told, he did not have time for."

"Did she ever get more than one crossword the same day?"

"She couldn't say. I think you're onto something there. It would be far too much of a coincidence if in all these months there wasn't even one day when she didn't receive more than one crossword. That surely points to cooperation between the sources."

"Did you find out who dated Jack Homer? And when?"

"During the last couple of weeks, Caroline dated him exclusively. Except the night that he died."

"Didn't she say she didn't date him too frequently?" asked Sylvia with a grin. "She said she 'gave him the privilege' once in a while although she was the employer and he the employee."

Mac smiled. "Oh, she was soft on him all right. I think she was getting him around to tying the knot."

"But didn't want to admit it."

"I think that is a sensitive issue. Would you admit it if you were in that situation?"

"I guess not," said Sylvia. "But I'd never be in that situation."

"So, Jack Homer was not the big cheese." Billy picked up the thread. "Did you determine if he was a source for the crosswords?"

"Yes, Paul did pick Jack Homer as another source. So we do have the link from Gloria Fairbanks to Jack Homer. But we can't go to trial with it. Gloria would probably swear in court that Paul was a source for her crosswords but Paul would not volunteer any information. His business, his reputation, perhaps even his life depends on his silence. He'll probably take the Fifth Amendment and hide behind his lawyer."

"Did you find out how many people sent messages through Paul?"

"No, he clammed up about that. I think he got some of his courage back. He said it was one thing to identify a dead person and something else to reveal his clients."

"But you weren't asking him to reveal his clients," said Billy. "Only the number of people who sent messages to Gloria Fairbanks."

"He wouldn't reveal that either. I think he is very protective about Gloria Fairbanks." Mac grinned. "Poor, lovesick puppy!"

"Perhaps I should have questioned him," said Sylvia with a wink. "He may have unburdened his soul to lovely me."

Billy went on to the next loose end.

"How about the security systems? Did you find about the company that installed those systems?"

"Yes, we did find about that. They were all protected by the same system. That was another good call of yours, son. I have asked the company to find out if there was a power outage anytime in the two weeks that the owners were on vacation. They must have logbooks with that kind of information."

"Oh, we can narrow it down from two weeks to the exact date, Dad. We can solve the crosswords and fix the date." Billy was excited. "Then it wouldn't be a coincidence as you mentioned this morning – it would be actual evidence linking Jack Homer and the crosswords to the burglaries."

"It is not evidence yet, son. It can still be called a coincidence. We don't have any evidence for sure that Jack sent those particular messages. We know from Paul that Jack Homer delivered some of the

Crossword Crimes

crosswords, and Jack Keegan delivered some others. We know from Gloria that some of the crosswords came from inside the newspaper office and others from Paul. We even know which ones were internal and which from Paul. However, we don't have the connection from Paul to Jack Homer. Paul would never reveal that. We wouldn't get the cross-reference between crosswords and sources from him as we did with Gloria Fairbanks. And not all the addresses put forth by Jack Homer have been burgled. Didn't you notice that only two of the three addresses you found were broken into?"

"What you're saying is that we cannot get any judge to give us a warrant to search the newspaper publisher or the distributor," said Sylvia. "Or subpoena Paul and get him to reveal all his sources. This is all circumstantial evidence and nothing to substantiate our case. I agree with you. However, it will be useful to get the information so that we can determine whether we are on the right track or not. I think that the children should solve the puzzles to narrow down exactly when the burglaries occurred. We can check that against the security logs."

Mac conceded.

"All right, go ahead, you three. Solve those puzzles and find out when the big boss gave the orders to do the burglaries. I'll give you the dates that the other victims were on vacation, and you can search for the 'Do it tonight' message within that period."

The three teens were thrilled. They had been assigned a duty as part of the investigation!

"Stand back! It's a job for the Solvers!" shouted Billy.

"Oh! Is that what you call yourselves?" asked Helen. She joined the group around the kitchen table.

"Yeah, Mom. Johnny and I started this group to solve all kinds of riddles, puzzles, and all kinds of posers. Emily joined us a couple of days ago."

"Yeah," added Johnny. "We solved the crosswords for this case."

"What case?"

"I'll fill you in later, dear," said Mac. "For now, I'll just say that these children are helping the police by finding messages hidden in crossword puzzles. They're heading out to the library to look at back issues of newspapers."

"You should also give some thought to your history assignment on the Normandy Conquest, Billy," Emily reminded Billy. "It's due Monday. You may be able to get some material at the library. You can look into that. Johnny and I can solve the crosswords. And I can help you put your report together later. Personally, I don't think you should do that report. Mr. Smith was too hard on you."

"Yeah," said Tommy. "Ten pages for falling asleep in his class. That's not fair."

"Did you fall asleep in class, Billy?" Helen asked sharply.

##

12. A LESSON IN HISTORY

"I didn't fall asleep," Billy protested, glaring at Emily and Johnny. "I was distracted. I was thinking about the case. Anyway, I never liked remembering dates and details about dead people."

"Don't you like remembering dates and details about dead people like Sir Isaac Newton?" Helen asked Billy with a knowing smile.

"That's different, Mom!" Billy protested. "He was a genius. He was a scientist, not a king or something."

"Would you be interested in the kings if scientists were involved in the story?"

"Like what, for instance?"

"Like how the Roman Marcus Claudius Marcellus was kept at bay by weapons designed by Archimedes. Or how Fibonacci discovered his famous number series when he was solving a problem posed by the king. Kings and statesmen have supported and fostered the growth of science."

"How does that help me?" asked Billy. "No scientist had anything to do with the Normandy Conquest."

"Don't be too sure about that. Have you heard of the Bayeaux Tapestry?"

Billy shook his head.

"I have," said Emily. "The Normandy Conquest is recorded on that."

"That's right. It is one of the sources of eyewitness record of the Normandy Conquest. There's a comet depicted on the Tapestry. Today, we all know that a comet is yet another celestial object. If we hear of a comet in the neighborhood of the earth, we eagerly scan the skies for it. In those days, it was taken as an ill omen. Soldiers who saw the comet feared that it signaled doom and disaster. There are historians who say that this led to a drop in morale, which could have been a major factor in favor of William, the Conqueror. This record of a comet on the Bayeaux Tapestry is significant. It was one of the sightings that Sir Edmund Halley took into account when determining the frequency of the famous comet named for him. And do you know whom Halley consulted for theories on orbits around the sun? Sir Isaac Newton!"

Billy was stunned. He stared at his mother in awe. She brought the subject back to his idol!

"Wow!" was all he managed to say at long last.

"Don't discount something as unimportant. History deals with development of thoughts and progress of civilizations as well as details about individuals and dates of specific events. The individuals are important because of their achievements which others have built or can build on, or mistakes which others ought not to make. If we can only learn from mistakes, we should not commit each one of those mistakes. Rather, we ought experience them vicariously and thus learn from others' mistakes. History is an account of mistakes as much as it is an account of achievements. People have achieved things by believing in themselves and what they set out to achieve. Be inspired by some of the achievements. Learn to believe in yourself. Learn to look at the world from a different perspective. Take Columbus as an example. There's an apocryphal story about him. Several of his critics met with him and pooh-poohed his discovery of the New World. They told him that there was nothing great about finding a New World. 'Anyone can do that,' they said. Columbus asked them to make an egg stand on one end. They all tried and failed. Finally, Columbus brought the egg down hard on the table. The end broke, and the egg stood on the jagged edges of the broken end. 'What's so great about that?' scoffed his critics. 'Anyone can do that.' 'Yes,' said Columbus. 'Anyone can do that. But none of you thought of it. I did.' That is what such people are famous for. They think of something that no one else thought of. Or look at the works of others in a new light. Einstein's Special Theory of Relativity is just that: He built upon the achievements of many great Physicists. That is not to say that it was not an achievement – it was a wonderful achievement. He achieved it with wonderful insight. And his General Theory of Relativity was an original thought far ahead of anyone else in his time. Even Newton said that he saw far because he stood on the shoulders of giants. Some thoughts are revolutionary, but most thoughts are evolutionary – they evolve from others. Even revolutionary thoughts are based on existing ideas but with a 'Quantum Leap', as Einstein called it, that skips a few stages of evolution. People add incremental ideas to an existing idea and make it grow slowly. Someone skips a step and makes it grow quickly. Then, it goes back to growing slowly again. The study of history is the study of progress and the study of thought. Understanding history will help you understand people and why they do what they do. It will help you anticipate their actions."

"Are you saying that even science has a history?" asked Billy.

"You said that you were not interested in kings or other non-scientists. Let me give you an example to show you the impact these non-scientists have had on us. Julius Caesar was not a scientist. However, he was impressed by the calendar that the Egyptians kept, and make Rome adopt that calendar in 46 BCE. That year had 445 days, the longest year in recorded history. His calendar included the concept of an additional day every fourth year, the concept of a leap year. There was a flaw in that calculation: Not every fourth year is a leap year. The earth's revolution around the sun is not completed in exactly 365 1/4 days. This correction was applied several hundred years later. Do you know who did that?"

"I know," said Billy, unexpectedly. Emily and Johnny looked at him in surprise. "Pope Gregory XIII. It was called the Gregorian Reform."

"And how did you know that?" asked his mother, with some surprise.

"The book that you gave me, Mom, the one about Sir Isaac Newton - It said that his birthday was given as Christmas of 1642, but was sometimes put in the first week of January because of the Gregorian Reform. I didn't understand what that meant, so I looked it up in the encyclopaedia."

Helen smiled at her little science freak. "Don't you see that if it involves something that you're interested in, you take the effort to understand it? Billy, textbooks give you raw information, and teachers are supposed to help you understand that information. But it is your task to learn. Each of us learns in a different manner because each of us is different and has different interests. It is up to you to determine the best way for you to learn. Since you are so interested in science, take something you must learn whether you want to or not, and associate that with Newton, or Einstein, or any of your heroes. That will get involved in that lesson, and it is easiest to learn when you get involved in something."

Emily looked at Helen with respect.

"Now I truly understand why everyone calls you the best teacher our school ever had. You don't teach – you help your students understand and learn."

Helen turned to Emily.

"Thank you, dear," she said. "There is something more I'd like to do. I'd like you children to learn to think. I don't mean to say that you do not know how to think now. But make a practice of thinking outside the box. Like the white queen said to Alice, think of twelve impossible things before breakfast. And broaden your knowledge base by reading about as many things as you can and understanding them. Internalize what you read. Then you can be truly creative. You can then take that 'Quantum Leap' that makes existing ideas grow quickly. You will leave a lasting impression on the world. Then you will be part of history that children in the future will have to learn about."

Helen turned back to Billy.

"When you write that report, don't look at the Normandy Conquest as an isolated event in history. History is not about isolated events. It is a continuous cascade where one event leads to another. As I showed you with the example of Halley's Comet, everything is interrelated. Pick up the thread much before the Normandy Conquest, and write of events that led to and that followed that event. You will see it in its full light and be able to explain its position in the grand scheme of history. For example, start with the Roman conquest of England and its impact, including the way lengths and distances were measured and the width of a cart track corresponding to the width of a Roman chariot. The Normandy Conquest was the last major conquest of England, and although the line of succession is not unbroken, except for the Whig Oligarchy, the line of royal leaders is fairly unbroken. You can find all that at the library while you're helping your father with this case."

Billy and the gang went to the library with the ranges of dates to find out when the burglaries took place. Mac and Sylvia followed up on the security people.

"Back again," greeted the librarian.

"Yes, ma'am," said Billy. "We're almost done with our research."

They split up, with Emily and Johnny looking up the dates and Billy working on his assignment.

"Look in the date ranges Dad gave," Billy told the other two. "You can skip the first four days since they'll probably be the address, the number of days, instructions to case the joint and a report on whether it was feasible or not. You'll probably find the 'Do it tonight' instruction on the fifth day or so."

"Yessir, Mr. President, Sir!" said Johnny with a salute. Emily giggled. They accepted Billy as their leader quite naturally – he *was* the smartest of the three, with the highest grades overall (although Emily *did* beat him at history). They took his instructions without resentment. It was not as though he was ordering them around. They were a natural extension of his appendages.

Billy took the librarian's help to research into the Normandy Conquest, the Bayeaux Tapestry and Halley's Comet for his report. He was still at it when Emily and Johnny finished their task and went looking for him. Billy was taking notes furiously.

"For someone who hates history, you've done quite some reading," remarked Emily, idly picking up one of the dozen books piled up next to Billy.

"'History through Pictures' ... That must be interesting."

Billy looked up from his notes.

"Yeah! That has an interesting picture of the Bayeaux Tapestry. Mom was right. Soldiers were shying away at the sight and horses were rearing in fear."

"Mankind has always feared the unexplained," remarked the librarian, hovering nearby. "Almost every ancient religion has venerated the elements. There have been gods of thunder, lightning and rain in the ancient civilizations. And comets have been considered omens of disaster for centuries. William Shakespeare's Julius Caesar said, 'When beggars die, there are no comets seen; The heavens themselves blaze forth the death of princes.' This is a very special comet, too. Halley's Comet has been the most celebrated comet in all history."

Emily and Johnny waited until the librarian was out of earshot and then showed Billy the information they had collected.

"We found them all, Billy," Johnny exclaimed. "In each of the date ranges your father gave us, we looked for a crossword with the hidden word 'Tonight'. These are the dates on which those crosswords appeared."

Billy quickly completed his notes.

"Let's go," he said.

"And about time, too," said Johnny. "At the rate at which you were going, I thought you were going to copy the entire textbook."

The three Solvers packed their materials and left.

#

It was late in the afternoon as Billy and his friends rode homewards. Their route took them past the park at the center of the town.

"Let's cut across the park," suggested Billy. "It'll be shorter."

So he thought!

They entered Elmwood's main park and followed a bike path that ran alongside the black top road. The road ended at a parking lot. The path continued and cut through the park. It wound along a little stream and snaked around clumps of bushes that bordered on well-manicured lawns.

In summer, the park was quite alive with games and picnics going on in every corner. As fall proceeded, there were only a few runners, roller-bladers and other exercise freaks, but by-and-large, the park was empty. And lonely. A perfect setting for an ambush ...

As the three teens rounded a particularly tall clump of bushes, they found their way blocked. A few large stones had been rolled onto the path. The three bicycles screeched to a halt.

"Well, well, well! Look who's here," called a nasty voice.

It was Boulder, perched on top of the pile of rocks.

As the trio turned around to go back the way they came, Ed and Mike, two of Boulder's cronies came around the bushes and cut off their escape route.

They had nowhere to escape!

They turned around to face Boulder again.

##

13. CONFRONTATION

Boulder held a short wooden club in his hand, and grinned maliciously.

Ed pulled Johnny off his bike and held him with one hand trapped behind his back. Mike held Emily's bike with one hand and Emily's wrist with the other. Neither Johnny nor Emily was going to run anywhere – they watched horrified as Boulder swaggered towards Billy, swinging his club lightly but dangerously.

"No Miss Andrews to go runnin' to, MacFarlane. No Coach Peterson to help you. An' if you run away, your precious friends are gonna get hurt. I've got you where I want you. You're gonna pay for every detention you cost me." Boulder was so happy he was actually skipping.

Billy let the bike fall from under him and stepped back. All he had with him was a little bag of books slung across his back, but he also had his training. And that was not going to fail him. He slipped his bag off and held it tightly between his hands. He kept his eyes on the club. He remembered the little rubber balls his father pelted him with during training. He compared the end of the bat with those balls – the bat would be much slower, but be packed with more force when Boulder swung it. His deflection would have to be perfect. He could afford to miss even once – one blow from that ape would be crippling.

Boulder swung the bat. Billy heard his father's voice echo in his head.

"Bring the paddle in line."

"Deflect the ball away from the body."

"Don't swing across the body."

Focusing every ounce of his consciousness, he blocked and deflected every one of Boulder's attacks. If he was able to evade the blow by ducking under it, stepping back or stepping aside, he did so. Boulder's face registered surprise – this was not what he expected. He expected no resistance. And he did not expect any difficulty in landing a few good blows with his club. He tried to feint, to thrust, and to swing wildly, but Billy was up to anything Boulder could dish out.

Other expressions changed, too. Boulder's cronies looked on, stunned. Emily and Johnny were initially apprehensive. Then, as they noticed how Billy was handling the situation, they cheered loudly every time Boulder attacked and was bested by Billy.

Boulder was all power and no stamina. Billy, with his training, was hardly strained, while Boulder was terribly out of breath. He grunted with every swing. Boulder was getting frustrated, too, and swung more and more wildly. And feebly. It was getting to be time to end the whole thing.

"There is no point in launching an offensive if there is a hole in your defense," his father had said. Boulder had no defense. He was launching an offense and was unprotected every time

Finally, Billy found the right opportunity.

Boulder brought the club down as though he was chopping wood. Billy stepped back, let the bag drop to one side, and brought his fist up from the ground until Boulder's chin met it.

"Don't hit at something, Billy," his father had said. "Hit through it. At the point of impact, your fist or leg must be moving at its highest speed."

Billy was a very good pupil. He threw his shoulder behind that punch – in fact, he threw his whole body behind that punch. He heard the thump and felt his fist jar. He felt a jab of pain shoot from his fist upon impact. He didn't stop – he kept going until he could go no more.

Boulder took a couple of steps backwards. He swayed for a couple of seconds. His eyes turned glassy and his knees buckled. Slowly, as though in slow motion, he crumpled and lay at Billy's feet.

"Timber!" said Billy, triumphantly. "The bigger they are, the harder they fall." He rubbed his knuckles tenderly.

Emily and Johnny cheered from where they stood.

Billy bent down and wrenched the club from Boulder's ineffective grasp. He turned towards where Boulder's cronies still stood holding their respective captives. They took one look at the prone Boulder, and at the club Billy now twirled in his hands, then at each other. Panic showed on their faces. Billy took one step forward. They dropped their hold on their captives, turned and fled.

"You were wonderful, Billy!"

"Yeah! You said that you were in training, but you fought as though you were fully trained!"

Billy grinned proudly.

"You could have run away, you know," said Emily.

"And let that animal hurt you? Never!"

"I know," smiled Emily. "You're loyal. You'd never let your friends down."

#

They quickly got home. Billy told his parents what had happened.

"Well, I hope that teaches him a lesson. He'll probably leave you alone from now on," said Mac.

They compared their findings from the crossword with the information Mac and Sylvia got from the security company.

"The dates match exactly," declared Mac.

But it didn't take them much further in solving the case.

"What else is common about the victims?" Emily asked.

"For one, they were all in Elmwood," said Sylvia.

"That's right!" said Johnny. "There's only a street address in the message. The town must always be Elmwood."

"For another, they were always independent, single-family homes."

"That's why they didn't break into the second place. That was a house with two families." That was Emily.

"And they all occurred at the same time of the day. The security systems were all tripped by power outages at around the same time of day – around five in the morning."

Billy was deep in thought.

"What's on your mind, Billy?" Sylvia asked.

"This sounds like a very well planned operation. Someone gives an address and the time that the address is vulnerable; someone verifies if that house has the right security system and is the right type; based on this information someone gives the go-ahead; someone fixes the security system; some breaks in and steals everything; someone splits the loot. Now, how many people are there in the gang? There are only two conduits – Paul and the big boss. Jack Keegan was creating and solving crosswords for the gang. Perhaps Jack Homer was creating his own. Was anyone else capable of creating crosswords? Or solving them?"

Mac nodded. "This is similar to the other question you had the other day, Billy. Why kill Jack Homer if he was the goose who laid golden eggs unless there was a new goose? I guess his goose was cooked," he added with a grin.

Crossword Crimes

"There may not be a replacement for Jack Keegan, Dad. If the killer of Jack Homer heard the message Jack Keegan left on the answering machine, then killed him to prevent him from spilling the beans to anyone else, I wonder if anyone else knows about it."

"You have a point there," said Sylvia. "I found some background on Jack Keegan. A few years ago, Jack Keegan was a part of another gang of burglars. He didn't like killing, so when the gang killed someone, he turned informant for the police. He received a reduced sentence for his cooperation, and relocated to this area after he was released. Someone who knew of his earlier days may have thought he would spill the beans and killed him."

"That gets back to another earlier question: who was the intended victim?" Mac added.

"Could Jack Keegan have been killed by any of the people he helped put away?" asked Billy.

"No, they are all still serving their sentences," replied Sylvia.

"Was there someone who didn't get arrested who might have killed Jack?"

"It's curious you should mention that," said Sylvia. "There was one person in the gang that Jack wouldn't help put away, and that was a girl named Goldie Fitzgerald. She was the leader's moll. Jack had a crush on her, and she was kind to Jack."

"What was she like?" asked Mac.

"My notes say that she was a very attractive platinum blonde, heavy on makeup and into motorcycles, leather jackets, leather mini-skirts and full length leather boots."

Platinum blonde!

"Caroline Fallace is a platinum blonde," said Johnny.

"You would remember details about Caroline," teased Emily. Johnny blushed.

"This gang used to operate across the country," said Sylvia. "Caroline has had her travel agency for five years right here, before Jack Keegan squealed on his gang the last time."

"The point in favor of Jack Homer as the intended victim is that Jack Keegan, who created and solved puzzles for the gang, called him to warn him. He probably wouldn't have done that if he thought that he was the intended victim," said Mac.

"He may have not been sure. He may have been on his guard, and, since he didn't like killing anyway, warned Jack Homer as well," said Billy. He paused. "I have a feeling we know all, or almost all, that we needed to know. Perhaps we should look at puzzles since Wednesday, since the one that said 'Kill Jack'".

"I'm afraid we don't have those newspapers, son," said his mother. "We sent them for recycling."

"We still have them," said Sylvia. "Our street recycles tomorrow."

"I'll get them, Mom," volunteered Johnny.

"Let's all go," said Billy.

And so the three youngsters left.

"I have today's newspaper," said Helen. "Let's look at it while we are waiting for them."

The three of them pored over the crossword puzzle together. Helen took on this task since the other two were not as experienced in solving crosswords.

"I see what Billy talked about," she said. "There are incidental words formed without any clues. Let's see..."

And the three of them looked at the words in horror. And then at each other.

"Kill", "the", "brats"!

Instantly, Mac rushed out to the car. He pulled the car out of the driveway with tires squealing, turned on his siren, and tore down the street. Meanwhile, Sylvia jumped to the phone to call her husband to check if Johnny got home all right.

Five minutes later, they all knew.

"They're gone," said Sylvia. The phone slipped from her hand. She stumbled over to the kitchen table and sat heavily. Helen went over and put her arm around her shoulders. The two women wept silently.

Mac burst in. His face was black as thunder. This was war.

"I've called Captain Ortez," he told Sylvia. "There will be a squad car here shortly."

As he spoke, sirens came wailing down the street. Captain Ortez himself came in the first car. Mac received him and brought him directly to the kitchen. The captain's eyes blazed.

"Mac, Helen, Sylvia. This is an outrage. I have put the entire squad on this detail. Everyone who is available is scouring the town for your children."

"Thanks, chief," said Helen, quietly. Her eyes were dry, but red. And her voice had that quiet resolve which Mac knew very well. The ever-smiling, gentle, affectionate Helen was more dangerous than a pit-bull when crossed.

The MacFarlane's kitchen became the base of operations.

The first thing that Helen did was to call David Richards. She told him briefly that his daughter was in trouble and asked him to come over. She met him at the door and brought him the kitchen. Between the three of them, Mac, Sylvia and Helen, they brought him up to date on the case and all that the children had done.

When he saw the clue in the crossword, he clenched his jaw tightly. His nostrils flared, his eyes burned and veins popped up on his forehead. He brought his ham-like fist on kitchen table, and said in a low, menacing voice:

"Sergeant MacFarlane, I'm sure you will find these people and bring them to justice. When you do, give me just one minute with the animal that lays a finger on my princess."

"Mr. Richards, I feel just as you do. For the moment, there is nothing we can do but wait. There are squad cars scouring the town, looking for clues, questioning witnesses, and trying to find our children. All I ask is that you wait here. This is the base of operations, and it is best that all be here tonight."

Sylvia's husband, Charlie Wu had joined them. Helen sent out for pizza to accommodate the crowd in the house. Sylvia, Mac and Captain Ortez huddled around a large map of Elmwood and a powerful CB radio, placing markers in different places as they heard from dispatchers and from squad cars. Helen, David and Charlie made small conversation and sipped coffee.

It was a long wait.

##

14. KIDNAPPED!

As the three children rode their bicycles towards Johnny Wu's house, a large, white van suddenly pulled in front of them.

"Run!" yelled Billy, but they were not fast enough. The van's doors opened, and several men quickly surrounded them. All the men were similarly dressed in black pants and black sweatshirts, and they all wore black ski masks. Billy tried to put up a fight, but he was no match for them. Working fast and efficiently, the men bound, gagged and blindfolded the trio, and bundled them unceremoniously into the back of the van. The men also threw the teens' bicycles into the van so as to leave no evidence of struggle. Then, they packed back into the van and sped away before anyone was the wiser. Since it was a quiet, residential neighborhood, enjoying a quiet Saturday evening, there were no witnesses. All the police found, when the asked around shortly afterwards, was from one man who was relaxing on his back porch. He had heard squealing wheels, and saw a white van speed away. He did not note the license plates, and couldn't describe the van any better, which did not help the police too much.

With his eyes bound, Billy strained his other senses to find out where they were headed. The van stopped speeding within a couple of blocks, perhaps not to attract any attention. Their kidnappers made several random turns and randomly accelerated and slowed down. Billy was confused by this maneuver.

After some time, the van stopped. One door opened. Billy heard a rough voice.

"So these are the brats that have been snooping around! They won't bother us for long. Take them to the river, weight their feet down and throw them over!"

Billy's heart froze at those words. He struggled in vain against the ropes that bound him.

Then, there was a whisper!

"Let me beat them up. Please ... Just once!"

Billy recognized that voice! It was Boulder! What was he doing here?

"Quiet!" hissed the first voice. "We don't have time to waste over your petty games!"

"Get going!" he ordered again.

The door slammed shut, and the van started off once more.

#

They were going to be killed!

Billy wasn't going to take this without a fight. He tried to stand up, but with his eyes blindfolded, and his hands bound behind him, he couldn't push himself up. He couldn't have lasted long on his feet anyway – they were bound, too.

Billy rolled over the floor of the van and came to a stop against a soft body. It was Emily. He twisted and turned so that his back was against her, and tapped her with his bound hands. She turned around and slid so that their hands met. Billy tested the knots on her hands. They were well tied.

If only he could see!

He used his shoulders and the movement of the van and crept upwards until his hands felt her hair, then the cloth that gagged her. He tested that. It was much easier to undo. He released the knot and slid up until he felt her blindfold. He released that, too. Finally, he crept down until Emily's hands felt his gag. Emily understood. She untied his gag, and then his blindfold.

"Are you all right?" Billy whispered.

"Yes," Emily whispered back.

Billy blinked a few times. His eyes were equally useless even without the blindfold! The inside of the van was pitch-dark. It was probably getting dark outside, as well. He could barely make out Johnny against a corner. The three of them were in the back of an empty delivery van. Their bicycles were heaped in the forward corner. The men who captured them all seemed to be in the cab of the van.

Billy turned his attention to the cords that bound Emily. He tried to pull the knot out with his teeth, but his braces got in the way. Working furiously, he bit through the rope, picking one strand of the nylon at a time and gnashing his teeth until it snapped. After what seemed like an eternity, he had one entire thickness of rope sliced. The knot loosened. Billy moved loops over the cut ends with his teeth, feeling the knot with his tongue and lips since his eyes were equally effective – or ineffective - with or without a blindfold in the dark van. Finally, the cord slipped and Emily had her hands free.

She quickly turned and worked on Billy's bonds. In much less time than it took to free Emily, Billy was free. But of course, Emily was working with much more sophisticated tools – hands – than Billy did – teeth! They undid the cords on their feet and stood up.

Emily hugged Billy and held him tightly.

"I'm scared, Billy!" Emily whispered.

"So am I, Emily. But as long as I'm able to stand on my feet, I will not allow those guys to hurt you. We have the advantage – those guys don't know we're free. Let's make the most of it and find a way to get away. Let's get Johnny free first."

The back of the van was bouncing too much for them to be on their feet long. They went down on their knees and crawled over to the corner where Johnny lay. Billy bent over his ear and whispered.

"Johnny, we managed to free ourselves. We'll get you loose."

Working together, Emily and Billy had Johnny loose in almost no time.

They went over to their bicycles. The bicycles were not damaged.

"What shall we do?" asked Emily in a low voice.

Billy went to the back of the van and felt the door there. He bent down and felt for a handle. He found it, and tried it. The door opened – at least they were not locked in. The kidnappers did not figure that the teens would be able to free themselves!

Billy stumbled back to the others.

"Stay here with the bikes," he instructed in a whisper. "I'll open the doors and come back. We'll need to ride backwards and leap out of the van. It may be dangerous. I don't think any vehicle is following us. Just keep your balance when you land, turn around and keep going."

He went back to the door and threw it open. As he had thought, there was no vehicle behind them. It was a clear, cloudless night, and the crescent moon cast a dim light on the landscape.

He quickly went back to his bicycle.

"Go!" he whispered.

The three of them mounted the bikes. Emily and Johnny followed Billy's lead. He turned his bike towards the front of the van and pushed it back with his feet. He waited at the edge, stabilizing himself against what felt like a bucking bronco. When the bounces subsided for a moment, he practically jumped back holding the bike with his knees. Upon landing, he fought to keep his balance. The bike moved forward due to inertia. Billy let it roll forward and watched as his friends copied him.

Emily came next. She kicked off from the end, but couldn't keep her balance. The bike bounced once, and then slipped from under her. Emily fell to her side, and rolled forward. Billy quickly moved up to her and stopped.

"Are you hurt?"

"I... I'll be okay. I couldn't hold on. I fell on my shoulder and arm."

Billy felt her shoulder and arm gingerly. Emily winced.

"Doesn't feel as though you've broken anything. I'll get the bike. See if you can ride it."

Johnny jumped next. He managed to keep his balance. He braked hard, then turned and rode to Billy and Emily.

Billy checked Emily's bike. It was dented but functional. The handlebars had moved out of alignment. Billy straightened it out. Emily mounted her bike and checked if she could ride it.

"My arm hurts, but I can ride."

"You will have to bear it until we're safe, Emily."

She agreed, and the three of them sped off. Peddling furiously, they came to a curve in the road and stopped. They looked back. The van was out of sight.

"Come on!" shouted Billy. "Let's keep going. It won't be long before they notice the doors flapping in the back. They'll notice us missing and back track. We must cover much ground before that."

There were no streetlights, but the almost full moon gave enough light for them to pick their way. In a few minutes, they came to an intersection. They made out the street signs – High Street and River Road

– but it meant nothing to them. They hadn't the slightest inkling as to where they were.

"Turn right!" said Billy. "I don't know where we are, but it may be better to take a side road than to stay on the main road."

High Street turned out to be true to its name – it climbed higher and higher. The youngsters were panting soon, even Billy who was in the best shape, but they all rode for their lives. Finally, High Street reached its high point, and they sped downhill.

"Should we turn into a driveway and knock on the door?" panted Emily.

"Let's see if we can find a pay phone soon. If we can't, then we can do as you say."

Finally, they reached another intersection.

"Which way?" panted Johnny. He was in no position to take decisions. His knees were shaking like jelly and his thighs felt very tight. His lungs were on fire.

"Left," said Billy. "We had turned right the last time. With all the twists and turns in the road, I am not sure which direction we are headed, but I don't want to go in a circle and land up where we started. We may come out right in front of them and get caught again!"

This was a wider road, about as wide as River Road. Perhaps they could hitch a ride.

They rode for nearly a half-hour. The going here was much easier than on High Street, but did not see any houses to try what Emily had suggested.

Finally, Johnny spotted something.

"A gas station!" he cried.

They sped towards it. It was closed, and dark.

But there, in the far corner, was a single telephone booth!

The phone rang at the MacFarlane residence. Mac walked wearily to it and picked it up.

"MacFarlane," he said. His voice sounded hoarse. He was tired, more emotionally than physically.

"Will you accept a collect call from Billy?" the operator asked Mac.

Billy! He could hardly believe his ears!

"YES!" he shouted.

He cupped the receiver and faced the rest of the gathering in the kitchen.

"Billy!" he whispered, but he needn't have. His face told them all they needed to know. Warmth was spreading again in that bleak atmosphere.

"Dad?" asked Billy's voice over the line.

"Billy! Where are you? Are you all right?"

"I don't know where we are, Dad. We managed to escape from the men who kidnapped us. I'm at a phone in a gas station, but I have no idea what town this is."

"Don't worry, son. Stay on the line. I'll have the call traced and get a squad car to you in no time."

Two minutes later, a police car turned into the gas station. About forty-five minutes later, the three children were eating a hot meal and drinking hot chocolate around the MacFarlane kitchen table while their parents were laughing, crying, hugging them and each other all at once.

"Don't ask the children any questions until they have had some rest," said Helen protectively.

"It's all right, Mom," Billy began, but Mac cut him off.

"I agree with your mother, Billy. You've all had a long and traumatic day. You should all get some sleep right now."

Billy remembered something.

"Dad, Mom, we escaped by jumping from a moving vehicle. Emily landed badly. She hurt herself."

Emily smiled gratefully at Billy.

"It's much better now, Billy. I think it's only a bruise."

Nevertheless, Helen took her up and checked her out. The shoulder and arm were mottled with purple blotches.

"Oh, you poor thing!" she exclaimed. She rubbed it down with liniment.

Helen brought down some sleeping bags so the children could camp in the family room. The adults went to their respective homes.

The eastern sky was getting lighter by the time they all got to sleep. Captain Ortez insisted upon having a patrol car constantly checking the three houses.

"The neighborhood's sealed tight," he told Mac before he left. "They'd be stupid to make another attempt tonight."

"We need to crack this case soon. We can keep those kids bottled up indoors while those maniacs are on the loose, but we can't keep it up forever."

"You must be close now," the captain assured him. "Why else would they attempt to pull off something as daring as kidnapping your son and Sylvia's boy? Something's bound to come up soon."

##

15. LIGHT DAWNS

The next morning, Billy came in to breakfast at 10 o'clock.

"Sorry, Dad," he said, sheepishly. "I overslept."

His father looked up from his notes and smiled.

"That was quite an adventure you children had, Billy. I'm surprised that you're up at all. The others are still asleep. Do you think you can answer some questions?"

"Sure!"

Helen got Billy some toast and orange juice, and sat down to listen to his narrative.

"Tell me what happened. I'll take notes and ask some questions as we go along."

"Well, as we were heading towards Johnny's house, this white van came from nowhere and cut us off. Some guys all dressed in black got out and grabbed us."

"Did you see where that van came from?"

"I thought I saw a van outside our house when we started out. I guess the three of us were very excited and quite engrossed in our discussion. The van must have followed us and cut us off when the coast was clear."

"Go on."

"The guys bound our hands behind us and tied up our feet. Then they gagged and blindfolded us and threw us in the back of the van. They also put the bikes in the van. I guess they didn't want to leave the bikes around. Then they sped off. I tried to count the number of turns they took, but I lost count. I don't know how long we traveled."

"Did they say anything to you?"

"The van stopped once, and someone said 'So these are the brats snooping around! Take them to the river, tie weights to their feet and throw them in.' No one said anything else."

Helen was horrified.

"Oh, my baby! I'd have lost you."

"I did warn you that this could be dangerous," said Mac, shaking his head. "Those guys killed twice in one night. They have no qualms about killing. And how did you escape?"

"The ropes binding us were quite tight, but the gags and blindfolds were easier to undo. I undid Emily's gag and blindfold and she undid mine. Then I chewed through the ropes that bound Emily's hands. After that, she was able to untie my bindings. We both freed Johnny. I was able to open the back door of the van from the inside. We got onto our bikes and jumped out."

Billy demonstrated the maneuver he used to jump backwards while holding onto the bike.

"Why did you do it that way, Billy?" asked Helen.

"Well, if we went head first, we would have fallen on our faces. Because of the law of inertia, we had to go in the direction of the van first, then turn around and go away. I learnt that from my physics lessons. And the book on Newton you gave me."

Helen looked at her son with pride.

"Billy, I'm proud of you. You have shown extreme courage and loyalty. And you did not lose your head when faced with a difficult situation."

"The danger is not past yet," said Mac. "I have some ground rules going forward. First of all, I don't want you stepping out of the house without an adult accompanying you until the case is solved. And I don't know if you should be involved in it anymore."

Crossword Crimes

"Don't you think it is a bit late for that, Dad? I'm up to my neck in it already. I almost lost my neck over it."

"You're right, it is too late. But I don't want you losing your neck anymore than you do. The rule stands about leaving the house without adult supervision. We may talk to your school about it if we need to."

"Do you mean I have to skip school until the case is solved?"

"No, you may not have to do that. But you won't go by yourself. Your mother or I will drop you and pick you."

"Aw, Dad! My classmates will make fun of me. They'll have a barrel of laughs at my expense."

"Better that than your funeral at my expense."

Billy softened. He came over and hugged his father. His father held him tight for a minute without saying a word. Mac generally held his emotions well, but felt them as deeply as any human being.

"Should we wake Emily and Johnny up?" Billy asked his mother.

"No, dear, they must be quite tired. Poor things! Let them sleep it off. I think the rest will do Emily's bruises much good."

#

Emily and Johnny awoke a bit later. Mac dropped them off at their homes so they could shower and get a change of clothes. They all assembled after lunch, including David Richards and Charlie Wu.

"I think we have all the pieces of the puzzle," opened Billy. "We just need to put it together."

"There's something else," added Sylvia. "At least one person, among all we have questioned, is lying. Who?"

"Let's do at the last thing we started out to do before we were ... rudely interrupted," suggested Emily.

Johnny had brought the crosswords from the previous days' newspapers. They huddled around and solved them.

"Here's what we have," said Sylvia. "'Jack', 'dead' on Thursday, 'Three nosy brats' on Friday. That must mean you kids. And 'Kill brats' Saturday."

"There's nothing in today's paper. All members of the gang might not know that the kids escaped."

"How did the gang know that we were looking them up?" asked Billy. "We didn't talk to anyone about it."

Emily corrected him.

"Johnny spilt it all to one person. The only person it was blurted to was Caroline," said Emily.

Johnny apologized. "I didn't mean to. I ... She surprised us, and I said the first thing that came to my head."

"You're dangerous around beautiful women," teased Emily. "We cannot give you secrets to keep. But we know how to extract information from you."

Johnny scowled at Emily.

"Let's start with Caroline," suggested Mac. "We'll take her in for questioning."

"If the chief allows it, bring her here," said Helen.

"What's on your mind?" asked Mac.

"I don't think she knows that the children escaped. If we present the children, and all of us – the children and their families - gang up on her, she may soften."

"It's worth a shot," agreed Sylvia. "Especially if she does not know that they are still alive. That would shock her."

They proposed it to Captain Ortez. He agreed. Several detectives went with Mac and Sylvia to the mall. Mac and Sylvia waited out of sight from the travel agency. Two other detectives approached Caroline Fallace and spoke quietly and earnestly to her. She came with them to where Mac and Sylvia were waiting.

"I was told you have some evidence against me, but wouldn't arrest me if I cooperated with you. What evidence is that? And what do I have to do to cooperate?" Caroline asked the waiting detectives.

"Please come with us," said Sylvia. "We have to show the evidence to you."

Caroline looked back towards the travel agency.

"I cannot leave my shop too long. I'm short-handed as it were. And this is a very busy time."

"It won't take long. And it is in your best interest to come with us."

"Do I need my lawyer?"

"Not now. And not at all, if you cooperate."

They took Caroline to Mac's car. Sylvia sat in the back with her while Mac sent the big car hurtling down the streets.

As they approached the MacFarlane home, Caroline looked around. They were in a very residential neighborhood, far from the center of town.

"Where are you taking me? I thought we were going to the police headquarters."

"Please be patient," said Mac. He pulled up into the driveway. They took her indoors. When Caroline saw the children, she froze in her tracks and stared at them. She turned around, but Mac barred her way.

"Are you surprised to see them alive?" asked Sylvia.

"I ... I don't know what you're talking about," Caroline blubbered, shrinking away from Sylvia.

"You're the only one who knew we were making inquiries about Jack Homer," said Emily, walking up to her.

"Yeah! I even told you that our parents did not send us," said Johnny, approaching her from another direction.

"This crossword clue could have only come from you," said Billy, waving the puzzle at her.

Caroline was stunned. She stared at Billy, and then at the crossword puzzle.

"You ... You know about the messages hidden in the crossword puzzles!"

"We've known for a while," said Johnny, airily.

Caroline's will was broken. She leaned against the wall and slid down to the floor.

"I never wanted to hurt you," she sobbed. "Trust me. I love children. I wanted to warn you, but I was afraid they'd kill me like they killed Jack. I've hated the gang ever since they killed my Jack."

She looked at the children, searching anxiously into their eyes. Billy looked coldly at her, but Emily knelt down and took one of Caroline's hands. Johnny followed suit (He would have been first, but held back to avoid being teased by the others). Caroline kissed them both, and Johnny blushed pink.

Caroline told them her side of the story.

"About a week ago, a woman came into my store and asked to see me. Jack had left for the day. I had never seen this woman before. She told me all about the crossword messages and what Jack had been doing for them for almost two years."

Sylvia was taking notes. "Can you describe the woman?"

"She was a platinum blonde, about 5 feet six inches tall, and buxom. She wore plenty of makeup. She wore a short leather skirt, some kind of frilly blouse and a leather jacket over it. Oh, yes! She wore long leather boots, all the way up to her thighs."

That was Goldie Fitzgerald, the woman whom Jack Keegan had protected before!

"Continue."

"She said that Jack had refused to work for them anymore. She asked me if I would do just what Jack did. She even taught me how to create the crosswords with hidden messages. It was a simple computer program she had created. All I had to do was enter the words of the message, and it printed out a crossword. I would be handsomely rewarded. Cash, as soon as the burglary was done. It would be hand delivered by a special messenger. And I had to go to the same messenger to deliver my messages."

The detectives looked at each other.

"Paul Samuels," said Mac.

"Yes, that was the special messenger."

"Go on," encouraged Sylvia.

Caroline continued, "Now I knew what they really wanted to do to Jack! They wanted to kill him because he'd refused to cooperate. After Jack died, I got really scared. I wanted to leave, but I didn't want to die like Jack."

"I guess you delivered your first message on Thursday, printed in the Friday's newspaper."

"I only meant to warn them about the children. I wanted to scare them. I did not mean the children any harm."

"Your message only mentioned that there were some nosy brats. How did they know whom to go after?"

"I got a telephone call on Friday. It was that woman. She wanted details, and I told her who the children were. I thought no one would hurt them since they were your children. I mean, with you being detectives and all that."

"Do you know other people involved in the burglaries?"

"No, my only contacts were that woman and the messenger. I don't even know if other members of the travel agency worked for the gang."

"We'll need you to give evidence when we get the rest of the gang in," said Mac.

"Am I to be arrested?"

"No. Not at this time, anyway. We can work out a deal," promised Sylvia. "In all fairness, your involvement with the gang is after all the burglaries and murders were committed. The only thing that could be held against you is the information leading to the kidnapping and attempted murder of the children. You're now cooperating with the law on that count, so there's nothing to hold against you."

Caroline was grateful. "I'll help you in anyway I can. But now, those people may try to kill me."

"We'll arrange for protection until we get the gang put away."

##

16. BILLY SPRINGS A TRAP

"Poor girl," said Helen, as Caroline left with Mac and Sylvia. "She got in way over her head. Still, she is the one who told them about you three. You cannot imagine how horrified I was when I saw those words 'Kill the brats' appear on the puzzle."

Billy jerked violently when he heard these last few words.

"What's on your mind, Billy?" asked his mother.

"I have it, Mom!" he exclaimed joyously. "I know who's behind the whole thing."

"How do you know that?" asked Johnny.

"By concentrating on the problem and not getting bowled over by beautiful women," said Billy with a sly grin. Johnny turned red again. They all laughed.

"I know how to save the town some money," said Emily. "We can seat Johnny at an intersection instead of the traffic light. Whenever we want the traffic to stop, we can shout 'Caroline!' and he'll turn red. When he recovers from that, the traffic can move again."

They all laughed again.

"I do say you have a good eye, my boy," boomed David Richards.

Helen steered the conversation back to the case.

"What were you going to say, Billy?"

"I know who killed the two Jacks, and who sent the message to kill us."

"Yeah, it's that mystery woman, the platinum blonde, Goldie Fitzgerald," said Johnny.

"Not so mysterious anymore," said Billy. "It has been staring us in our faces and we haven't seen it. Sort of hiding in plain sight. Like the messages in the crosswords."

"Who is it?" asked Emily persistently.

"I don't want to name any names yet," said Billy. "I want to set a trap and capture that person."

"Now, don't you do anything dangerous!" warned David. "I've had enough of a scare to last me a while."

"No, sir, Mr. Richards. But you may have to."

"Me? What can I do?"

"With Caroline's cooperation, we can set up a message. I would like you to deliver the message. Paul Samuels has never seen you, so you are a believable source. And you can ask him a few questions."

"You're playing this hand close to your chest, son," boomed the big man. "Are you sure you know what you're doing?"

"Yes, I do," Billy's voice rang confidently.

When Mac and Sylvia returned, Billy explained it all to them.

"I don't know, son," said Mac. "What if the killer doesn't take the bait."

"Trust me, Dad. The killer may not know that the code has been broken."

Caroline agreed to cooperate.

"I would do anything to make up for putting those bright kids in such a spot," she said. "And I need to avenge my Jack's death, too."

"Was he your fiancé?" Sylvia asked her.

"No. But I was going to ask him."

With Caroline's acceptance, Billy wrote a new message. They put it through the software to create crosswords. It was quite a complicated one because he had many words to hide.

"What are the hidden words?" Emily asked him.

Billy showed her.

"Brats escape meet park seven."

"Are you going to be at the park?" asked his father.

"I have to. I need to confirm something. But I won't be alone. We'll all be there."

"What was the question you wanted me to ask the messenger?" asked Emily's father.

"Mr. Richards, this message is for Gloria Fairbanks of the Elmwood Gazette from Caroline Fallace. From what my father told me, I think Paul Samuels has a crush on her. When you give him this package, if you keep on about how beautiful she is, and ask him if he's seen her recently, he might confirm a suspicion I have."

"Aren't you going to share your suspicion with us?" David asked him.

"No, sir, not at this time. This is only one half of the picture. The other will be at the park tomorrow evening. Also ask him about the platinum blondes. Caroline gave her a message on Thursday. If he talks about another platinum blonde, we know who that may be."

Mac nodded. "Goldie Fitzgerald. Jack's moll."

"No," said Billy, "she was Jack's old gang's leader's moll. She may have been more than that to Jack." He turned to Emily's father. "Please ask him if the platinum blonde gave any message for anyone other than Gloria Fairbanks yesterday."

#

David Richards did not need much of a disguise. He tousled his hair, discarded his pipe and wore a pair of faded jeans and an old tee shirt that he used for chores about the house. Sylvia gave him directions to Paul Samuels' office. Billy had prepared the package as Caroline had asked him to. Mac put in the hundred dollars for Paul's fee.

"I hope the chief sees this as a necessary expense and reimburses me," he said.

"If he doesn't," said Sylvia with feeling, "I am willing to split that with you. Putting away those monsters who almost cost me my child will be well worth it."

David went to Paul Samuels' office alone. Mac and Sylvia followed him a little distance behind, and there was a sniper on the opposite roof in case there was any danger to David.

"For Gloria Fairbanks from Caroline Fallace," David told Paul as he signed for it. And sighed. "What a beautiful woman." He sighed again. "I wish I were delivering that one myself. I guess you must be happy about these messages. Gives you the opportunity to see her once in a while."

"Yes," said Paul. "I gave her several last week."

"Yes," agreed David. "The platinum blondes."

"Yes, the platinum blondes," Paul continued. "Caroline Fallace and Goldie. I was angry when Goldie said yesterday that the package was not for Gloria Fairbanks." As usual, he enjoyed rolling his tongue over the name. "You could have knocked me over with a feather when she told me it was for George Sanders. I didn't want to see that big ugly gorilla. I wanted to see Gloria."

You could have knocked David over with a feather, too. Billy's idea worked – he was able to pump Paul for information. He thanked Paul and left.

#

David shared all he had learnt from Paul with the rest of the group.

"Goldie! That would be Goldie Fitzgerald," exclaimed Sylvia. "She was part of the gang Jack Keegan worked with before."

"George Sanders!" Billy exclaimed at the same time. "Would that be Boulder's father?"

"Yes, son," said Mac. "That's another piece of the puzzle. George Sanders owns one of the newspaper distribution outfits here."

"I heard Boulder's voice when we were being kidnapped," said Billy. "I forgot about that until now. He whispered, 'Let me beat them up.' I guess he was sore about being beaten up by li'l ol' me. Dad, you did mention that all the burglaries occurred about the same time in the morning. George Sanders' newspaper distribution company does most of the work in the morning. It would not be unusual to see one of his trucks parked on a road for about a half-hour. I'll bet that's how it is done."

"Whom do you expect to trap tomorrow?"

"Goldie Fitzgerald. The mysterious platinum blonde."

"Do you expect Sanders and his cronies?"

"Probably not. Without Jack Keegan to solve the crossword, the crew would not know about the rendezvous."

"Let's take Sanders in today. That'll leave us Goldie for tomorrow. I'm anxious to get these dangerous people off the streets."

"Dad, if you take in the newspaper distributors, won't people notice. That may scare Goldie Fitzgerald away."

"Good point. I'll get someone to handle that angle. We'll get Sanders, but keep it under wraps and have the newspapers distributed by another crew."

#

Billy and his friends went with Mac and Sylvia up to George Sanders' warehouse.

"Hello, Sanders," said Mac, coolly, when they came upon him.

"MacFarlane!" George Sanders scowled. "What the hell are you doing on my premises?"

"Official work, Sanders. Otherwise, I would be caught dead in a rat hole like this. I want to question you about some kidnapping and attempted murder."

"Don't know what you're talking about," was the sullen reply. Several of the men formed a human wall behind George Sanders. One of them displayed a large wrench menacingly, another wound a length of chain around his bulging forearm. Boulder walked up and stood by his father. Billy was delighted to see his swollen jaw.

Billy went up to his father and whispered something in his ear. Mac nodded. He took out a small portable tape recorder from his jacket, displayed it for all to see, and put it on record mode.

"Billy, here, recognized one of your vans outside. He also recognized your son's voice."

"Did he say he saw my son?" asked George Sanders with an unpleasant grin. "Can he pick him out of a line-up?"

"No, I didn't *see* him," said Billy.

"Of course, you didn't," scoffed Boulder. "You couldn't see anything through those blindfolds."

"Be quiet!" yelled George Sanders.

But it was too late!

"How did you know Billy was blindfolded?" asked Mac. "Very few people knew that – the people who kidnapped these children and the people they told their story to. Since you were not around when they told their story, it goes to show that you were there at the kidnapping."

"Get them," shouted Mac at his men.

They moved forward ...

... And froze!

"I'd love to see you try it," Sylvia said, waving her .38 Glock Police Special.

Mac called in for back up.

Captain Ortez arrived, too, along with David Richards.

"Let me at them," growled the big man. Mac restrained him.

"Easy, now. The law will take care of them."

Captain Ortez had brought along a search warrant. The detectives quickly searched through the huge warehouse and found some of the stolen articles.

"Do you think all of them were involved in the burglaries?" Mac asked Billy.

"I think we can find one of them, for sure," Billy replied. "We can cross-reference this newspaper distributor's payroll records with the security company. The person or persons who came from there knew how to defeat the security system."

At this, one of the men came forward.

"I'm not going back inside the slammer," he said to Captain Ortez. "I'll tell you what you need to know."

"Pete, you stinking rat!" yelled Sanders. "You squeal, and I'll get you when I get out!"

The man looked disdainfully at the Sanders pair.

"I've had it with your yelling and your bullying, you sourpuss," he declared.

He told his story.

"My name is Peter Carmody. I used to work as an installer of the security system. About five years ago, there was a big electrical storm in this area and many of the security systems were damaged due to lightning and power surges. At that time the company developed a defensive mechanism. If the security system detected a very high surge of electricity, it shut itself down for about fifteen minutes. This was reported as a power outage in the log. It turned out to be a flaw in the security system. When they introduced the feature, they tested it by simulating a power surge. They had this piece of equipment. You had to attach it to the power line, turn the crank and throw a switch. It would cause a power surge and the system would shut itself down. I borrowed it for a couple of days and had a friend of mine duplicate it. Then I found a way of tapping the main power line to a house with a kind of clamp that pushed a needle into it. With these two things, I could create a powerful spike. We then had fifteen minutes to ransack the place."

"How did you know if the house had the right kind of the burglar alarm?"

"The company had upgraded all their clients to at least that version a couple of years ago. It was better than being sued by clients after electrical storms."

"They are going to be sued anyway when news of this flaw in the system hits them," remarked Captain Ortez.

"How many of Sanders' employees were involved in the burglaries?" asked Sylvia.

"All of this bunch, and a couple who're not here right now. We went in the newspaper delivery van, so no one would suspect. I mean, it is normal to see a news delivery van early in the morning. The boys would get in position and give me a signal. Then, I'd shut down the alarm and give the signal. Benny there's a lock picker. He'd have the door open in a trice. Three of them would go in and get all the loot. We'd be out of there in ten minutes."

"How about the kidnapping? Do you know who did it?"

"Only those four." Peter pointed the men out.

"Book them!" said Captain Ortez.

The entire crowd, including Boulder, who played a small part as a lookout during the burglaries, was taken into custody. They would be indicted on seven counts of breaking and entering, and seven counts of theft and larceny. Additionally, the four men Peter pointed out were booked on three counts of kidnapping and three counts of attempted murder. George Sanders, as their leader, was booked on all counts, and more - conspiracy. Boulder, as a minor, would be sent to juvenile courts.

"That's a long list of charges. They will be behind bars for a long time," said Mac. "If all the charges stick, their grandchildren will have grandchildren by the time they're out."

"We'll make sure the charges stick," said Captain Ortez.

George Sanders glared at the three kids as he passed them.

"I knew you three brats were trouble. I should have finished you when I had a chance!"

17. TRIUMPH

The next day was Monday. Mac took charge of dropping all the three children at school.

"Don't you even step out without an adult with you!" he warned. "I have informed Miss Andrews about the situation. She will ensure proper supervision and protection for you three. Either Sylvia or I will pick you up at the end of the day, after your track training."

The school was a-buzz with news about Boulder's arrest. Billy and his two friends knew all there was to know about it, but were sworn to silence. The killer was still on the loose, and the case was not yet closed. They smiled smugly at each other when they heard the latest rumor.

"Boulder was part of a gang that killed 37 policemen."

"They used the news trucks to transport the bodies."

The two boys who were with Boulder when Billy knocked him out seemed to have spread the word about Billy's triumph. Boulder's supporters avoided Billy all day. Many students who hated Boulder and his strong-arm tactics congratulated Billy.

"Heard you knocked Boulder out with one punch, Billy."

"Good job!"

"Billy flattened Boulder with one blow!"

"Billy, the Boulder Smasher!"

Rich Welles and his bunch glared at Billy.

#

The hours did not pass fast enough for Billy. He looked at his watch every few moments. Once he compared his watch with Johnny's to see if it was running slowly, or had stopped. The only thing of note that relieved his excitement was the history class.

With the information he got from the library, with all that his mother had told him, and with Emily's help, Billy wrote a twenty-five-page report. He placed it on the table before the teacher arrived. Billy watched nervously as George Smith picked it up and glanced through it cursorily.

"Didn't I assign you a ten-page-report?"

"Yes, Mr. Smith."

"Did you fall asleep when I assigned it?" Mr. Smith smiled sardonically. The class tittered. Rich Welles smirked. "Is that why you wrote more than I asked you to?"

"No, sir. It was very fascinating. I gathered so much information that I had to cut out portions otherwise it would have become a fifty-page-report."

His teacher's eyes narrowed. He looked at Billy with suspicion.

"Since when have you been interested in history?" he asked. "You've never shown any interest in my classes. Leopards don't change their spots. Are you playing games with me? This report had better be authentic, or you're in deep trouble. I'll go through it right after class so if I have to give you a week's detention, it can start today." He paused. "In fact, I'll do better than that. Come up here and read the report out to the class."

Rich Welles laughed triumphantly, and some of his supporters smirked and sniggered.

Billy walked confidently up to Mr. Smith. He took the report from his teacher, opened it and read it in a clear, loud voice. His passion for what he had written flowed through him. Within a minute, almost the entire class was hanging on to his every word with

Crossword Crimes

rapt attention. The exceptions, naturally, were Rich Welles and his confederates.

When Billy finished his reading, the class applauded, George Smith the loudest.

"That was wonderful, Billy! I have changed my mind about you. You are, indeed, the star student in this class. That report gets you full marks for all assignments for the course. You need not turn in any assignments. If you do out of your own interest, you get extra credits."

Rich Welles was livid. His supporters sulked. The rest of the class cheered Billy.

Billy thanked Emily for her help with the report.

"You're welcome, Billy. How about a *quid pro quo*? Now, you can help me with math."

#

After school, Sylvia picked them up and dropped them all off at Billy's house.

"Stay here," she told them. "Mac and I will come for you at six."

Again, time passed very slowly for Billy. At five, his mother brought in some sandwiches.

"I don't know when you'll have dinner tonight. This'll keep you going."

By a quarter to six, the three teens were pacing anxiously by the front door.

Mac's big car pulled into the driveway.

"Here he is!" shouted Billy. They gathered their jackets and rushed out to meet Mac and Sylvia.

"Ready?" asked Mac.

"Are we ever! Let's go!"

"A few words first: I want you all to promise you will not do anything rash or dangerous."

The trio promised. They drove down to the park, the same one where Boulder and Billy battled. They met a squad of policemen at the entrance.

"All set?" asked Mac.

"Yes, Sergeant," one of them replied. We'll call you on the radio the moment we spot her."

Caroline met them at the park. She, the detectives and the children concealed themselves among a clump of bushes and waited.

At seven, a platinum blonde entered the park. One of the policemen saw her and called Mac on the radio.

"She's moving towards the fountain in the center of the park."

Soon, she came into view. She stopped near the fountain and looked around.

She was as Caroline had described. She wore a form-fitting short leather skirt, dark leather jacket and long leather boots.

"That's her all right," whispered Caroline.

Billy whispered something into his father's ear. Mac nodded and tapped Sylvia, and the three of them headed out.

"The rest of you remain here," whispered Mac.

They split up. Billy walked directly towards the blonde. Mac and Sylvia fanned out. They had their weapons in their hands.

"Hello, Goldie. Or should I call you Gloria?" said Billy. "Were you expecting Caroline Fallace? George Sanders won't be here. There's no one to solve the puzzle for him. And he's been arrested anyway."

The woman spun around and stared at Billy.

"So you're the brat responsible for the breakdown of my well-laid plans. Too bad. I came to settle matters with that double-crossing Caroline, but you're getting yours instead."

She put her hand inside her handbag and pulled out a .38 with a silencer at its end.

"Hold it!" called Mac, from her right. He had a steady bead on her. "Drop that weapon!"

"That goes double from me!" called Sylvia, from her left.

The blonde looked from one to the other. Slowly, she lowered her arm. She let the weapon slip to the ground.

Mac spoke into his radio. Soon, several police officers had gathered around the blonde. She was searched for more weapons and then handcuffed.

"When did you know?" Gloria asked Billy.

"Yesterday. It took me a while but I finally put it all together. If I could figure out that the puzzle had hidden words, how long would it take a veteran crossword editor? If a kid like me could spot the hidden messages, a pro like Gloria Fairbanks ought to know what was happening. I figured that you must have known what was going on. It clicked yesterday morning when two things happened. First, Caroline mentioned that the platinum blonde that inducted her into the gang taught her to make the crossword puzzles with the hidden messages. Second, my mother mentioned that she solved Saturday's puzzle and found the hidden message. If it was so easy to teach someone how to create messages, and if it was so easy to find the messages, how come the person in charge of crosswords didn't stumble on it for eighteen months? I figured you must be part of the gang."

"How did you figure out that Gloria Fairbanks and Goldie Fitzgerald was the same person?" she asked, removing her wig.

"Little things, really. But they made sense. The burglaries began eighteen months ago, the same time as Jack was released on parole. If Jack had a soft corner for Goldie Fitzgerald, he would home in on her when he was released. She would also have to occupy a key position in whatever he did. There is no Goldie Fitzgerald in this area. Could she have taken on another identity? The only woman in this operation until Caroline was inducted was Gloria Fairbanks. Gloria held a very important position in this operation. Could she and Goldie Fitzgerald be one and the same?

"Goldie has not been seen here much, and that's saying much. I mean – look at you: You would stand out in any crowd in that outfit. I'm sure you do that deliberately. But Goldie Fitzgerald appeared twice in the past week, so she must be here somewhere. The first time was to induct Caroline, the second to send a message to George Sanders to dispose of my friends and me. Both those decisions could only come from the boss. We know from solving the crossword messages and from cross-reference that the instructions came from within Elmwood Gazette and all reports came through Paul. Goldie Fitzgerald has never been seen at Elmwood Gazette, but Gloria Fairbanks works there. Paul Samuels was a courier on the wrong side of the law. Yet, he was more than a mere messenger as far as Gloria Fairbanks was concerned. He had been captivated and cultivated by her. Is this how Goldie Fitzgerald wielded influence over Jack Keegan's old gang? I have read that when someone takes on a new identity, there is an attempt to keep the old initials. Here we Gloria Fairbanks and Goldie Fitzgerald with the same initials 'G.F.'."

"You're smart. I underestimated you. So you broke the crossword code. Did you create the puzzle Paul brought me yesterday?"

"Yes. Just as Sherlock Holmes solved the code of the Dancing Men and wrote a message in that code. It was fun. Caroline let me use your software."

Caroline and the others emerged from their place of concealment.

"That's her, all right," spat Caroline, her eyes blazing with all her pent up emotions. "She killed my Jack!"

She looked like she was going to pounce on Gloria. Sylvia held her back, although she felt Gloria could take Caroline on if she wanted to. With her long association with crime, Gloria was probably well versed in ways of defending herself.

Billy noticed the engagement ring on Gloria's left hand.

"You must have felt bad about killing your fiancé," observed Billy.

"Jack was her fiancé?" asked Caroline incredulously.

"I'm talking about Jack Keegan. That must have been the price of getting off the hook in the old place."

Gloria nodded.

"He was always soft on me. When he turned in the old gang, I begged him not to turn me in. He asked me to marry him, and I agreed. I did like him anyway, although while the gang was still functional, and I was known as the leader's moll, it couldn't happen. In a way, it's good the old gang broke up."

"Jack Keegan turned his old crowd in because of a killing. But he didn't turn the killer in. That's ironic," said Sylvia.

Gloria turned to Sylvia in surprise. "How do you figure that?"

"That's easy. You've killed twice easily, and had no qualms about killing again. You gave instructions to kill three children, and you were going to kill Caroline. Just this evening, you tried to kill Billy. You are a killer, there's no question about that. You must have been the killer in the old gang. It shouldn't be hard to figure out. All we need to do is ask the so-called leader of the old gang. I'll bet he knew your role as a killer."

"I'll save you a trip. I *was* the killer there. That's how I kept the so-called leader, as you called him, in check. He was quite scared of me. He tried to kill me once, but I charmed the man he sent to do the job. Now he's so terrified that he won't say a word against me even to save his skin.

"Well, it was good while it lasted," Gloria said, philosophically. "I ought to have quit while I was ahead. But the temptation to pull off one more coup kept me on. And I tried different ways. I'd have quit this one in another year if Jack hadn't rocked the boat. The kingdom is lost, all for the want of a horseshoe nail."

"It was a good plan," Mac agreed. "I do give you credit for your ability to create a good scheme and carry it out. You could have used your skills for good purposes. Unfortunately, you're on the wrong side of the law."

"Do you have anything to add to what we know?" asked Sylvia.

Gloria thought for a minute.

"You know most of it anyway. I'll fill in the details. With all the things you know, I'll probably be in for a long time anyway. It wouldn't hurt me anymore to tell you everything."

##

18. TYING IT ALL UP

Gloria told her story.

"You're right, I'm the brains behind this gang. The guys didn't have half a brain between them. Except Jack Keegan – he could use his head, that one. I was the brains behind the old gang, too. I pretended to be the moll of one of the men. The others thought that he was the leader, and he knew better than to open his mouth and spill the beans. Jack Keegan was one of the boys there. He was actually quite sharp. He had a crush on me, and I enjoyed his company. One of the boys in the old gang was getting restless, and I had to silence him. Jack didn't like that killing, so he went to the cops. He went to jail so he'd be safe from the gang. I hadn't expected that from him. Anyway, he didn't know that I had done the killing since he thought that I was only decoration there. He didn't have the slightest idea that I was the brains behind the whole thing. I met him in his jail cell and begged him not to name me as a gang member. He agreed conditionally – he asked me to marry him. I agreed, so he didn't turn me in. I moved to Elmwood after the old gang collapsed. I didn't want to be there anymore."

"How did you get a job as a crossword editor at Elmwood Times?" asked Sylvia.

"So there are things you don't know," Gloria gloated.

"I know!" said Billy, suddenly. "You had a double life in the old place too! You must have worked at creating crosswords there, too."

"That should be easy to verify," said Mac. "One phone call should do it."

Gloria was disappointed. She'd lost her edge.

"How did you figure that out?" she asked Billy.

"You gave it away. You did not worry that any of the other members would squeal on you. Maybe Jack was the only one who knew your alter ego. And I bet you created the software that makes puzzles with hidden messages."

Gloria shook her head in amazement.

"Serves me right! I've learnt never to underestimate kids."

"Did you use the crossword messages earlier?" asked Sylvia.

"No, I worked that out while Jack was in jail. In the old place, I used software to help me create crosswords as part of my job. I learnt how it worked and wrote my own version. It had a flaw in it – it failed to generate some of the clues, even if it fit the words in the right places. I discovered the flaw and turned it to my advantage. It became the perfect way of passing messages.

"I kept in touch with Jack during his incarceration. After Jack was released, he came directly to me. In the meantime, I found Paul Samuels and his unique messenger service. I found out about George Sanders and his gang of thieves from Paul. As Goldie, I approached George and mentioned this scheme – that I would tell him which houses would be empty and for how long, and he could burgle the joint and share the loot with me. He already had Peter Carmody and Benny the lock picker. They knew when a house would be empty because the owners stopped their newspapers for that time. They had pulled of some small jobs before, but got quite close to being caught a couple of times. Sometimes people stop newspapers for other reasons than being out of town. I told him that my scheme would be quite low risk and he grabbed at it."

"I suppose you told him that you worked for the big boss."

"That's right. I have found that criminals don't quite like to be led by a woman. In the old place, I had asked someone else to be the titular leader and passed myself off as his moll. That placed me in his hands, so to speak. As I mentioned earlier, he's scared enough of me to take the rap, but it's still a gamble. I didn't want to go through that problem again, so I invented a fictitious leader and passed myself off as his moll."

"Had you found Jack Homer by then?"

"They happened about the same time. I figured I could use a travel agent as the guy who tipped us off as to when a house was ripe for breaking into. I thought of cruises since the person is guaranteed to be away while the cruise is in progress. I was scouting around travel agencies for a suitable mole. I found Jack Homer. The poor sap was deep in gambling debts and was quite happy to do this for me. I put the whole plan into operation when my Jack was released from prison. I introduced him to George as the person who'd carry messages both ways. Even my Jack did not know that I was the person at the top. He thought that messages came to me from a higher source. He thought that I was someone's moll again. That hurt him because he didn't like the idea of me being with someone else. Since he knew of my dual identity, I promised him that soon Gloria would be his and his alone.

"Everything went smoothly until about three weeks ago. Jack Homer had this inflated view of his charm, and kept badgering me for a date. I'd always told him that I was engaged, and was not available for dates. Then one day when Jack Keegan had to go out of town on an errand, and I felt rather lonely, so I gave in to Jack Homer's persistent requests and dated him.

He'd only known me as Goldie. Sometime during the date, my wig slipped. He noticed that and pulled it off me. He recognized me as Gloria. He figured it was something he could blackmail me with. He demanded a bigger role for himself. He threatened to go to George Sanders and tell him that there was no Big Boss, that I was manipulating everyone. I still insisted that I was not the person giving instructions. I devised the exchange between myself and the Big Boss, and the Big Boss' instructions to kill Jack. I went up to his apartment on that day, showed him that puzzle and the instruction in it. First, I tried to scare him. Jack was not convinced. Then I pretended to give in to his demands. I suggested a little drink to seal the deal. I got Jack drunk and killed him. Then, as I was cleaning up the place to get rid of any evidence of my presence, Jack Keegan called. After hearing his message, I headed out to his place. I knocked on his door. He would not open. I called out to him. I don't know how and when he realized then that I was the killer in the other place as well. He escaped through a back window and climbed down a pipe. I saw him run past and called him from above. He refused to stop – he said he was going directly to the police to tell them about my involvement in both the crime gangs. He had the crossword puzzle in his hand. I didn't want to kill him, but I had no choice. I shot at him from above and hit him, but he kept going. By the time I came down the stairs, he had disappeared. I first went towards the airport but had no luck. Then I turned and drove the other way. I saw the sharp bend in the road and looked over the end on a hunch. I saw him and went down to him. He was dying. I saw the crossword in his hand and tore it from his grasp. You cannot imagine how upset I was when the police came with it the next day. I thought you were only trying to match a scrap of

Crossword Crimes

paper you found at the crime scene. I had no idea you solved the code until you all showed up today."

Mac beamed proudly at his son.

"That was my son's work. Not only did he crack the code, he put all the pieces together. We have George Sanders and his crowd, we have Caroline, although she's on our side now, and now we have you."

"Well, that's that!" said Captain Ortez. "Case completely closed. I think we have tied up every loose end. Two murders, seven unsolved burglaries and one unreported breaking and entering. The mayor is going to claim he was responsible for everything! You two can give me a complete report tomorrow." The last piece was directed at Sylvia and Mac. "Now, come on! I'll treat you all to a round of ice cream."

#

The mayor was quite pleased with Billy and his friends for their involvement in solving the murders and salvaging his reputation. He insisted that Captain Ortez reward them for their help. There was a special ceremony.

Young Billy – or, to give him his moment, William Thomas MacFarlane, Jr. – stood smartly with his back erect and head held high as Captain Ortez of the Elmwood Police Department pinned a special medal on his chest. Without turning his head, he found his parents, Detective Sergeant Wm. MacFarlane and Helen MacFarlane proudly cheering on. Out of the corner of his eye, he caught sight of his friends Emily Richards and Johnny Wu who were also being honored by the Police Department. Finally, he looked Captain Ortez straight in the eye.

"Good work, Billy!" boomed the big captain. "You and your friends helped the Police Department in nailing the Crossword Gang!"

"Thank you, sir!" said Billy, clearly and loudly. "Awfully glad to have helped."

#

And so ended the Solvers' first adventure. They solved other mysteries, and had other adventures. But those are subjects for other books.

Crossword Crimes

Made in the USA
Lexington, KY
07 February 2017